Dear Readers,

Many years ago, when I was a kid, my father said to me, "Bill, it doesn't really matter what you do in life. What's important is to be the *best* William Johnstone you can be."

I've never forgotten those words. And now, many years and almost two hundred books later, I like to think that I am still trying to be the best William Johnstone I can be. Whether it's Ben Raines in the Ashes series, or Frank Morgan, the last gunfighter, or Smoke Jensen, our intrepid mountain man, or John Barrone and his hardworking crew keeping America safe from terrorist lowlifes in the Code Name series, I want to make each new book better than the last and deliver powerful storytelling.

Equally important, I try to create the kinds of believable characters that we can all identify with, real people who face tough challenges. When one of my creations blasts an enemy into the middle of next week, you can be damn sure he had a good reason.

As a storyteller, my job is to entertain you, my readers, and to make sure that you get plenty of enjoyment from my books for your hard-earned money. This is not a job I take lightly. And I greatly appreciate your feedback—you are my gold, and your opinions *do* count. So please keep the letters and e-mails coming.

Respectfully yours,

William W. Johnstone

BOOK YOUR PLACE ON OUR WEBSITE AND MAKE THE READING CONNECTION!

We've created a customized website just for our very special readers, where you can get the inside scoop on everything that's going on with Zebra, Pinnacle and Kensington books.

When you come online, you'll have the exciting opportunity to:

- View covers of upcoming books

- Read sample chapters

- Learn about our future publishing schedule (listed by publication month *and author*)

- Find out when your favorite authors will be visiting a city near you

- Search for and order backlist books from our online catalog

- Check out author bios and background information

- Send e-mail to your favorite authors

- Meet the Kensington staff online

- Join us in weekly chats with authors, readers and other guests

- Get writing guidelines

- AND MUCH MORE!

**Visit our website at
http://www.kensingtonbooks.com**

WILLIAM W. JOHNSTONE

CODE NAME
EXTREME
PREJUDICE

PINNACLE BOOKS
Kensington Publishing Corp.
http://www.kensingtonbooks.com

One

Los Angeles, California

John Barrone, the field leader of the Code Name Team, despised drug pushers. When John was still in college, his younger brother had gotten hooked by a slick-talking punk, and died a couple of years later after shooting up with a hotshot. The law never did anything to the punk who hooked him and supplied him with the dope.

John's father, a wealthy banker, was driving home from work one night when he got caught in the middle of a gang war. He was killed by a burst of automatic-weapons fire. The shooters were never caught; no one was ever punished.

John's kid sister was mugged by a doped-up punk. She lay in a coma for sixteen weeks before she died. She left behind two small children, a very angry and bewildered husband, and half a million dollars in hospital bills her insurance didn't pay. The man who mugged her walked, because the eager young cop who arrested him did not read him his Miranda rights.

As a result of John Barrone's personal experience with drug pushers and users, he developed a very simple solution for solving the drug problem in America. If it was up to him, he would kill all the drug dealers, the growers, the drug lords, the pushers, a sizeable number of defense lawyers, and all the violent gang members. He would do it without reading them their Miranda rights, without worrying about sensitivities, and without trials. He would summarily execute them, and he wouldn't give a damn what color any of them were.

Because of John's philosophy about drug dealers, and because of his personal involvement in the case, he did not miss one day of Pablo Bustamante's trial.

Pablo Bustamante was a first-generation American, born of Colombian parents. It was widely believed, though never proven, that Pablo's father, Arturo Bustamante, was the one who assassinated President Jorge Eliecer Gaitan in 1948, thus starting the cycle of violence in that South American country in which over 300,000 were killed.

Arturo emigrated to America in 1962, wrangling a visa because of his strong anti-Communist beliefs. He brought two million dollars in cash with him, the seed money for the international drug cartel he started. When he was gunned down by a rival drug lord in 1994, his son, Pablo, took over.

Over the years, Arturo had managed to build a very powerful network of judges and politicians to keep him out of jail. Pablo inherited that network, and added to it by his high-profile association with show business and sports personalities. As a result, he considered himself invulnerable, and indeed, though the FBI, DEA, and state enforcement agencies suspected him of everything from extortion to procuring to drug dealing to murder, no grand jury had ever managed to bring an indictment against him.

That all changed, however, when McKenzie Dickens, a motion picture producer, was found shot to death in his office. The police had been unable to solve the crime, but a friend of the producer, a very wealthy financier who also happened to be one of the backers of the Code Name Team, asked the Team to take a hand. The Code Name Team succeeded where the police had failed, and Pablo Bustamante was charged with murder.

Bustamante's trial was a national sensation, with gavel-to-gavel coverage by Court TV and the World News Network. Although none of the high-profile actors or actresses were called to testify, many people who were in the movie business—writers, assistant directors, cameramen, grips, gaffers—did testify that cocaine and heroin, as well as some of the more exotic designer drugs, were in great abundance on the set of Dickens's movie, which was called *Stranglehall.*

The star of the picture, Jason Godfrey, missed so many days of shooting because of his drug habit that the picture was going way over budget. Many of the prosecution witnesses testified that they had overheard Dickens and Bustamante having a very bitter argument. Bustamante was one of the investors in the picture, and was using that leverage to gain entrée to the set. Dickens accused Bustamante of using that entrée to provide drugs to the cast and crew, thus slowing down production and causing the film to go over budget.

Shortly after John Barrone and the Code Name Team came onto the case, John learned that the homicide detective in charge of the criminal investigation was not only on Bustamante's payroll, but was actually the one who killed Dickens, on Bustamante's orders.

The detective agreed to turn state's evidence in exchange for a lesser charge. His testimony had been damning, backed up not only by his word, but by the revelation that he had been wearing a wire during his discussion with Bustamante.

"Why did you wear the wire?" the prosecutor asked during her examination.

"As insurance," the detective replied. "I thought that if I had taped evidence that he had ordered the hit on McKenzie Dickens, I would be safe."

"Safe from who?"

"Safe from Bustmante."

"Did you have authority for the wire?"

"Yes, ma'am," the detective replied. "Because of an on-going investigation into Bustamante's drug trafficking, there is a blanket warrant authorizing the use of phone taps, e-mail searches, and the wearing of recording equipment when in his presence. I was within the letter of the law when I was wired."

The prosecutor rested her case at nine o'clock the next morning, and Judge Ernest Westphaling turned to the defense counsel.

"You may present your closing arguments," he said.

Corey Livingston, Bustamante's lawyer, stood. "Your Honor, if it please the court, defense will waive its right for closing argument."

The courtroom gasped in shock.

"What?" the judge asked, the tone of his voice expressing the surprise of everyone in the court.

"I have no closing argument, Your Honor."

Like everyone else in the courtroom, John was puzzled by Livingston's comment, and he leaned over to whisper to Jennifer Barnes, the other Code Name Team member in court, who had helped him with the investigation.

"I don't like this," he said. "There's something wrong."

"Counselor, if you hope by your refusal to give closing argument to force me into declaring a mistrial, you may disabuse yourself of that notion. Now, you will give a closing argument."

"Very well, Your Honor," the lawyer said. Clearing his throat, he walked up to the bar to address the jury. "Ladies and gentlemen of the jury. Every bit of evidence you heard against Mr. Bustamante was illegally acquired. Therefore you cannot use it. And without the evidence, and without Detective Moore's testimony, there is no case against my client. You will have no choice but to find him not guilty."

The lawyer returned to the defense table.

"Ladies and gentlemen of the jury, you are to disregard everything counselor for the defense just said," Judge Westphaling declared in an irritated tone of voice. "I have admitted into evidence every people's exhibit and witness. Therefore you may consider it in weighing the guilt or innocence of Pablo Bustamante."

"Shit," John said under his breath.

"What is it?" Jennifer asked. "The judge just explained that the evidence can be used."

"Something is up," John said. "I don't know what it is, but something is up and Livingston knows it."

"Prosecution, closing arguments," Judge Westphaling said.

Laurie Cornet addressed the jury.

"Ladies and gentlemen of the jury. During the past several days, we have shown you . . ."

As the prosecutor continued her presentation to the jury, a young woman came into the courtroom and walked over to the defense table, where she handed Livingston an envelope. Livingston read it, smiled, and showed it to Bustamante, who read it and also smiled. Bustamante and Livingston embraced.

"Would the prosecution please suspend?" Judge Westphaling asked.

Surprised, Laurie Cornet looked over. "Yes, Your Honor, of course."

Westphaling looked at the defense attorney. "Mr. Livingston, perhaps you would be so good as to share with the court the basis of your celebration?"

"Yes, Your Honor, I would be glad to," Livingston said. He held up the envelope. "I have an order here from the Ninth Federal District, invalidating every piece of evidence the prosecution has introduced. In other words, Your Honor, prosecution has no case, so I intend to ask for a directed verdict of not guilty."

"What? Your Honor, may counsel approach the bench?" the prosecutor requested.

"Just a moment," Westphaling said as he saw one of his own messengers come into the courtroom. He signaled for the messenger to approach. The messenger did so, then handed the judge an envelope.

The judge looked at the envelope for a moment, then said, "Counselors, in my chambers. And, Mr. Barrone. Would you join us as well, please?"

"Here it is," John said under his breath. "The shit is about to hit the fan."

Most in the gallery had no idea who John Barrone was, and they looked on in curiosity as he rose from among them and disappeared through the door at the back of the courtroom.

"Mr. Barrone, when you were interviewing Detective Moore, did he have a lawyer with him?"

"No, Your Honor. I didn't deem that necessary. I was interviewing him, not interrogating him."

"You didn't deem it necessary," the judge repeated. "What about his Miranda rights?"

"Judge, I'm not a policeman. I was not under any obligation to read him his rights."

"You are not a policeman, Mr. Barrone, but there was a police officer present," Judge Westphaling said. "And any time there is a policeman present, the suspect must be read his Miranda rights."

John looked confused. "What policeman was present?"

"Correct me if I'm wrong, but at the time of your first interview with Detective Moore, he was a police officer."

"Wait a minute!" John asked, understanding now where this was going, but totally shocked by the implication. "Judge, are you saying that Detective Moore should have read the rights to himself?"

Judge Westphaling held up a letter. "No," he said. "I'm not saying that at all. But the Ninth District of the Federal Court is saying someone should have."

"A mistrial? After all this, you are declaring a mistrial?"

"I wish I could declare a mistrial. But I can't. So what I am declaring is a directed verdict of not guilty."

Pablo Bustamante and his lawyer were mobbed by reporters as they left the courthouse. John and Jennifer were on the front steps as well, joined by others from the courtroom, watching the drama of the press interviews.

"Mr. Bustamante, do you have any comment, sir, on how the trial turned out?"

"Yes," Bustamante replied. "I am only glad that my father was not alive to see the lengths to which some government officals will go to carry out their personal vendetta. As Senator Harriet Clayton herself said in a recent speech, my father's fight for democracy kept Colombia from going Communist.

"After the unpleasantness in Colombia, my father emigrated to America, where I was born. He loved his adopted country, as much as I love this, my native country.

"This trial was a waste of time and the taxpayers' money. I never should have been brought to trial in the first place, and I am happy that a jury of my peers has found me innocent."

"It wasn't exactly the jury that found you not guilty,"

one of the reporters reminded him. "The judge directed the verdict."

"Nevertheless, I am exonerated."

A long black limousine slid quietly to the curb in front of the courthouse and a very beautiful woman got out and ran to Bustamante. They kissed and embraced as the cameras clicked and rolled.

"Who is that woman?" Jennifer asked.

"Her name is Amber D'Amour," John replied. "She is Bustamante's girlfriend."

"Amber D'Amour?" Jennifer asked. She laughed. "You mean to tell me that someone actually is named Amber of Love?"

"She didn't start out with that name," John said. "She was born Alma Jackson. She picked up the name Amber D'Amour when she became a porn movie star."

Waving at the crowd, Bustamante hurried out to the car, held the door open for Amber, then slid in beside her. The car pulled away from the curb with Bustamante inside, a free man.

"Mr. Livingston, do you have anything to say?" one of the reporters asked Bustamante's lawyer.

"Yeah, how do you feel about using dirty tricks to get a murderer off?" another added. "Doesn't it bother your conscience?"

"No, it doesn't. I am a lawyer and as such, I am ethically and legally bound to represent my client in the most effective way possible."

Livingston looked around, and seeing that John Barrone was standing up toward the top of the steps some distance away from the others, he pointed.

"If you want someone to blame, there he is. It is cowboy mercenaries like him who have made a shambles of our legal system. They disregard the law for their own purposes . . . generally money . . . and we all pay. This time his cowboy tactics contaminated every piece of evidence he touched, and that ultimately left the prosecution without a case."

Waving triumphantly at the reporters and cameras, Livingstone hurried down to the curb where his own car waited.

Laurie Cornet was a small woman, but full of the spirit and fire that had caused her to get convictions or settlements on forty-one of the forty-two cases she had tried. The forty-second case was the one she had just completed.

"Miss Cornet, in a recent speech by Senator Harriet Clayton, she called Pablo Bustamante's father, Arturo, a latter-day Simon Bolivar, and she credited him with being one of the heroes who prevented Communism from taking root in South America. Do you think her comments may have hurt your case?"

"I would hope not," Miss Cornett answered.

"But you must know that there are some people who feel that Pablo Bustamante is a target of repeated investigations because of his father's political connections," the reporter insisted.

"Yes, well, let's talk abut Arturo Bustamante, shall we? His name was invoked several times by the defense during the trial just completed, and I was unable to respond. But neither legal procedure nor prosecutorial ethics restrict me now, so I would like the American people to know a little something about this man Senator Harriet Clayton hails as a modern-day Simon Bolivar.

"Arturo Bustamante called himself a freedom fighter. As a freedom fighter, his army would cut off testicles, slash open pregnant women's bellies and kill their unborn children. They developed something called the *corte corbata*, a way of cutting the throat that would leave the tongue hanging from the neck. He had people quartered, skinned, or slowly carved into pieces. They raided villages and farms until the streams and rivers ran red with blood.

"Then, after extorting millions of dollars from the innocent and terrorized people of Colombia, all couched in the guise of a fight against Communism, Arturo Busta-mante moved to the United States, where he was received with open arms."

"Are you saying he wasn't fighting Communism?"

"I'm saying ninety percent of his victims had never even heard of Communism."

"Will you attempt to retry the case?" one of the other reporters asked.

"Why should I?" Laurie Cornet replied.

"To seek justice."

"Unfortunately, we now have a federal court system that has such a slavish devotion to the letter of the law that they have lost sight of the intent of the law. That makes it impossible to find justice."

"Do you think—"

"Thank you," Laurie replied with an abrupt wave as she walked away from reporters who continued to scream unanswered questions at her.

On board American Airlines Flight 2427 LAX to DFW

One of the nice things about working with the Code Name Team was the opportunity for travel. Their assignments took them all over the world, and though sometimes they might have to travel by camel, they frequently enjoyed first-class travel. Such was the case today for John Barrone and Jennifer Barnes as they sat in the wide, spacious seats of first class.

"What are the poor folks back in cabin class eating?" John quipped as he carved into his veal Parmesan.

"Pretzels," Jennifer answered, taking a swallow of her wine.

"I've seen a few times when pretzels would seem like a feast," John said.

"True," Jennifer agreed. "John, I'm sorry."

John looked up from his plate. "Sorry?"

"About the trial. I know you really wanted to put Bustamante away."

"Not wanted, *want*," John corrected. "And we'll get him. Trust me on this, Jennifer. We will get that son of a bitch."

"Did you see Harriet Clayton's comment about the trial?"

"No."

"It was in the paper this morning."

"What did she have to say?"

"Wait, I'll read it to you," Jennifer said, reaching for the folded-up paper. She opened it to the column and began to read. "'An overreacting right-wing administration has caused an erosion of individual rights throughout our society. As a result, harsh, and sometimes jarring, action must be taken. If the government had a real case against Pablo Bustamante, they should have been able to make it without denying him his basic rights. I applaud the Ninth District Federal Court for their courageous stand in defending individual freedoms.'"

"What a crock of shit," John mumbled around a mouthful of food.

"What a piece of work she is," Jennifer said. "You know what I think?"

"What?"

"I think we should have left that bitch in the Sitarkistan Desert."

Two

Sitarkistan Desert, one year earlier

As John Barrone and the others of the Code Name Team took Harriet Clayton to the oasis, they were met by a swarthy, smiling man.

"Greetings, greetings," he said. "My name is Bilal. I am your driver and guide." Bilal extended his hand and John took it.

"I'm glad to see you," John said. "I knew the arrangements had been made, but you never know how things are going to turn out when there are third parties involved."

"I have been here for hours," Bilal said.

"Have you seen anyone?"

"Seen anyone?"

"Kadar may have come this way."

Bilal shook his head. "No, I have seen no one."

"We should get in touch with Don and tell him we made the connection, don't you think?" Mike Rojas asked.

"Yes," John answered. He looked at his watch. "But it is another five minutes before the satellite is in position."

"We should have used the geosynchronous satellite," Linda Marsh said.

John shook his head. "We couldn't. That one is dedicated to DOD use only. They would have picked us up fast, and shut us down."

"Don couldn't have found a way to get around that?"

"I'm sure he—"

"John. John, this is Don, do you copy?" Don's voice suddenly came through the earplugs of all of them.

"Don, yes, I copy," John said. "I thought we had another few minutes of blackout."

"We do. I'm tapped into the DOD satellite," Don said.

"You're on the Defense bird? Must be something hot for you to blow our cover like that."

"Hot enough, I suppose. You guys better find some cover fast. You're about to be attacked from the air."

"From the air? Whose planes?" John asked. "You aren't trying to tell me the Muhahidin has an air force, are you?"

"They're our planes," Don said.

"Well, call them off."

"I'm trying. You can listen in, if you want."

"Yes, give it a shot."

"This is a message for U.S. warplanes in Sitarkistan on a strike mission for Bathshira," Don said. "Abort your attack. I say again, abort your attack. You are about to attack friendlies."

"Who is this?" a voice asked, obviously one of the pilots.

"I'm a friend," Don said. "Abort your attack."

"What is the recall authenticator?"

"I don't know," Don admitted.

"You don't know, buster, because there isn't one. Nice try, towel-head. Now get off the air."

"No, I'm pleading with you. Do not attack. Do not attack. You will be attacking friendlies."

"I said, get off the air."

"U.S. Air Force pilot, this is John Barrone. I am the leader of a group of American mercenaries. We have rescued Senator Harriet Clayton. If you attack, you will be putting her in danger."

The Air Force pilot chuckled. "Mister, whoever you are, you are just giving me more incentive to attack."

"I told you who I am. My name is John Barrone."

"Well, Mr. John Barrone, if you are in the target area, I suggest you get your head down. I have strike orders and I intend to follow those orders."

"What are we going to do, John?" Chris Farmer asked.

"We're going to do what the man said," John said.

"What is it? What is happening?" Harriet asked. She had no earplug and therefore had been able to hear only one side of the conversation. "Is someone about to attack us?"

"I'm afraid so," John said. Looking toward the northwest, he saw them, four airplanes coming fast. "Here they are," he said. "Find someplace to get down."

"What?" Harriet said. "This is ridiculous. I am a United States Senator! What is going on here?"

"Senator, you'd better get your ass down, or get it shot off," Jennifer Barnes said sharply.

Little flashes of light appeared under the nose of each of the approaching planes. These were the Gatling guns, and a second after the flashes began, the bullets began whizzing by, snapping through the trees and bouncing off the rocks around them.

"Take cover!" John shouted, leaping behind a rock formation.

Harriet didn't have to be told a second time. Screaming in panic, she also ducked behind some nearby rocks.

The airplanes roared overhead at that moment, each of them dropping something that tumbled through the air as they came down.

"Napalm!" John shouted.

The bombs hit all around the oasis, erupting into huge blossoms of fire. John could feel the searing heat of the blasts, but fortunately, neither he nor any of the others were in any of the blast areas.

The planes made a high, sharp turn, then came back. This time they were firing rockets and the rockets began exploding all around the people on the ground. One of the rockets hit the Land Rover, and it went up with a roar.

"Do something!" Harriet screamed. "Tell them to stop!"

"You heard me try, didn't you?" John asked.

"You didn't try hard enough," Harriet insisted.

"Well, if you think you can do any better, lady, you try," John said.

"John, wait!" Jennifer said. "That's it! Let her try!"

"What?"

"She's a famous person," Jennifer said. "A pain in the ass, but famous. Maybe the pilot will recognize her voice."

"Yeah," John said. "Yeah, that's a good idea." John took off his lavaliere mike and handed it to Harriet. "Tell him to stop."

"How do I make it work?"

"I've set it to voice activation," John said. "Just speak."

Harriet nodded, then looked directly at the little microphone. "Listen to me, American pilot, whoever you are," she said. "This is Harriet Clayton, United States Senator from New Jersey. Harriet Clayton. You do know who I am, don't you?"

"I know who Senator Clayton is," the American pilot replied. "How do I know you are Clayton?"

"Listen to my voice, you Neanderthal military asshole!" Harriet said sharply. "Surely you have heard it before."

"Abort the attack," the voice said. "This is either Senator Clayton, or someone who does a very good impression of the bitch."

"What? What did you call me? What is your name, mister? I demand to know your name!"

The four airplanes made a low pass over the oasis, flashing by in absolute silence for just a second, the silence then followed by the thunder of their engines. They wagged their wings as they pulled up and started away.

"Mr. Barrone?" the pilot's voice said.

"Yes."

"This is Colonel Joe M. Anderson. I apologize for the mix-up. I'll have a rescue helicopter dispatched immediately."

"Thanks," John said.

Washington, D.C., the present

The Washington press corps was gathered en masse in the Senate cloakroom. Lights were bright, TV cameras were in place, microphones had been tested and now sprouted from the podium, and newspaper and magazine reporters stood by with narrow tablets and poised pencils.

In her office, Senator Harriet Clayton, junior Senator from New Jersey, sat with her campaign manager, Henry Norton.

"You will have served only four years of your first term," Henry told her. "But our polls indicate that the people of New Jersey will forgive you for not serving your full term if you are elected President."

"Yes, well, if they don't, piss on them," Harriet said. "I'll be running for President of the United States, not of New Jersey. And you said yourself that now was the time to act."

"Yes, your adventure in the desert last year has brought you a lot of publicity, all of it favorable. You went there with good intentions, you were taken hostage, and endured the ordeal heroically until you were rescued."

Harriet's communications coordinator stuck his head

into the office. Senator, it's nearly time for the broadcast, and the Vice President isn't here yet."

"You mean the former Vice President, don't you?" Harriet asked. "And don't bother waiting for him, he won't be here."

"Oh, I can't believe your husband wouldn't want to be at your side when you make the announcement," the communications coordinator said.

"We didn't tell him," Henry said.

The coordinator looked surprised for a moment, then nodded. "Oh. All right. Well, we have been given live time by over half the networks, so we need to leave now to take advantage of that window."

Harriet stood up, looked at her reflection in the mirror, then primped a bit. "How do I look?" she asked.

"Like the most beautiful president this country has ever had," Henry said.

"I don't know. There are some who will say that honor belongs to JFK," Harriet quipped as they left her office.

"Ladies and gentlemen, the junior Senator from the State of New Jersey, Senator Harriet Sinclair Clayton!" the communications coordinator shouted as they entered the Senate cloakroom. There were some cheers and a scattering of applause from the spectators, but the press corps made no demonstration. Harriet walked directly to the podium.

"Good afternoon, ladies and gentlemen of the Washington press corps, and to my fellow citizens across the United States.

"When the previous administration left office, our economy was strong, we were at peace, and we enjoyed the respect and cooperation of our allies and friends around the world.

"Now we are engaged in a war with no end in sight. Our economy is a shambles, and Americans of all political persuasions are feeling a sense of disconnect with their government. Therefore, I have come here, to the Senate cloakroom, where both John F. Kennedy and his brother, Bobby, announced their intention to run for President. I do so with full awareness of the historic symbolism of this place, and with absolute confidence, tempered by humility, that I am the best person for the job. Ladies and gentlemen, I hereby declare my candidacy for the presidency of the United States of America."

Again there were cheers and applause from her supporters, who had been strategically scattered through the room.

One of the reporters raised his hand.

"Senator, you seem to be suggesting that the current administration has taken us to war. But don't you think the terrorist activities of the last few years have, in fact, brought about that condition? I mean, you yourself were nearly a victim of the terrorists."

"Yes, I was," Harriet said. "I went to the Middle East in order to see if we could not come to some sort of understanding."

"Is it correct, Senator, that you went there without our government's sanction?" one of the other reporters said.

"That is true," Harriet said. "And that, I believe, is the principle reason for the failure of my mission. Had the government been fully behind me, had the current administration given me the authority to negotiate, things would have turned out differently."

"Do you really believe that, Senator? As I recall, Douglas Sharbell was killed within moments of your initial meeting, and you had to be rescued."

"Yes, and let me ask you this. Who do you think it was that rescued me?" Harriet asked.

"I beg your pardon?"

"Who rescued me?"

"Well, I'm not sure. I assume it was some joint operational force of the military and CIA."

"Well, you assume wrong, sir. The government did nothing to rescue me. On the contrary, the government sent the U.S. Air Force to conduct an air strike against me. I'm sure they were hoping to be able to shut me up forever."

"Then who did rescue you?"

"An elite team of privately funded mercenaries," Harriet said. "They call themselves the Code Name Team."

"Who, or what, is the Code Name Team?" someone asked.

"They are people who work just outside all legal restraints. While there are certain constitutional, or international, rules that restrict government operations, the Code Name Team blissfully ignores them."

"Senator, you sound critical of them, yet by your own admission, they saved your life."

"There are cases when principle is more important than a person's life," Harriet said. She held up her finger. "Besides, their way doesn't always work. It was their ham-handed, no-holds-barred investigation tactics that recently caused the Bustamante case to be thrown out of court."

"Do you—" one reporter started to ask, but Harriet interrupted him.

"Thank you, that is all," she said. She rushed from the cloakroom then, ignoring several more shouted questions.

For those watching across the United States, the picture on the screen returned to the various network studios, where earnest-looking male and female news anchors and commentators were prepared to begin their instant analysis. The World News Network was one such example.

There, Lauren Day, news anchor and host of *American Afternoon,* sat with political commentator Chet Benedict.

Lauren smiled at the camera. "Well, there you have it. All speculation has come to an end as Harriet Clayton has just announced that she is running for President. There are certainly no surprises there, as this has been expected ever since her husband's unsuccessful try in the last election. And of course, speculation greatly intensified after her dramatic rescue. Chet?"

"You are quite right in that her announcement for President has come as no surprise," Chet Benedict replied. "However, there was one rather startling piece of information to come out of her announcement. Up until now, it had been assumed that her rescue was pulled off by a special-forces-type military unit. Now we learn that that isn't so. Instead, she confirmed the existence of an ultra-secret, quasi-official team of mercenaries."

"You are talking about her reference to the—let's see, what did she call them?" Lauren asked, consulting the notes before her.

"The Code Name Team," Chet said.

"Yes, the Code Name Team. What is the Code Name Team? I don't think I've ever heard of it."

"Most people have not heard of it," Chet said. "But rumors of their existence have been floating around for sometime now. So far, though, they have only been rumors, not unlike the rumors of aliens and an intact flying saucer in Area Fifty-one. Today, for the first time, we were given firsthand acknowledgment of their existence."

"Is this Code Name Team a government operation?" Lauren asked.

"Nobody really knows," Chet replied. "But the best educated guess is that they are not a government agency, although their activities are sanctioned by, and sometimes even encouraged and aided by, the U.S. Government."

"Why would the U.S. wish to encourage and help a mercenary group?" Lauren asked.

"Well, think about it. A civilian group, free of governmental restraints, is also free of agreements and delicate arrangements. That means they can cross borders without causing an international incident."

"Then it is entirely possible, is it not, that despite Senator Clayton's insistence that the government had nothing to do with her rescue, they may have in fact employed this Code Name Team to do the job for them?"

"Yes, that is possible. And if so, Senator Clayton may have done great damage by exposing the existence of the group. If such a group does exist, I can't imagine they are very happy with her."

Code Name Team Headquarters, southwestern Texas

Because they were between missions, the entire Code Name Team happened to be in residence at their headquarters, a sprawling house in the desert of southwest Texas. The house was so secret and unapproachable that they sometimes referred to it as Area Fifty-Two, a joking reference to the top-secret Area Fifty-One. There were very few people who knew about the Code Name Team. Fewer still knew what it was, and only the most trusted could name its members.

The Code Name Team was an extralegal, rather than illegal, group whose job it was to "handle" things that fell through the cracks of legal technicality. The team was created to take care of those dregs of society—the terrorists, murderers, drug-dealers, etc.—who too often got away with their misdeeds because of misguided liberal guilt over the normal inequities of nature.

Although the Code Name Team had no connection

with the government, Chet Benedict was correct in his assessment that they were sanctioned, and often helped by, the government. There were a few highly placed individuals in the government who knew, and privately appreciated, what the team was doing.

Because of the super-secret nature of the team, its members had no family or social life. They had no future, and they had burned the bridges to their past. There was more than one way into the team, but there was no way out, short of a body bag. The men and women of the Code Name Team were teammates, coworkers, fellow warriors, friends, and family in and of themselves.

Those few times they were able to come together without a specific assignment were rare, and when they did come together, they managed to find ways to unwind and relax.

As several sides of pork ribs were barbecuing over a mesquite fire, the members of the team were spread out around the residence. Some were out on the patio, kicked back and drinking beer. Two were engaged in a game of chess, while Mike Rojas and Chris Farmer were taking turns throwing knives at each other, trying to see how close they could come without actually hitting.

Mike Rojas was Mexican-American, and though his family had maintained its Mexican heritage, Mike was quick to point out that he had an ancestor who'd been at the Alamo.

"Big deal," Chris replied when Mike mentioned that the first time. "If I recall my history, there were a lot of Mexicans at the Alamo."

"Yes, but my ancestor fought on the side of the Americans," Mike said.

It was Mike's time with the knife, and he threw it at Chris. The knife whizzed by and pinned Chris's shirt to the wooden wall behind him. "That counts as a hit," Chris shouted. "Ten points off."

Chris Farmer was a trained Army sniper who, during the first Gulf War, had compiled a record of seventeen confirmed kills, not one from closer than one thousand yards. When Senator Harriet Clayton was a hostage of Abdul Kadan Kadar, it was Chris's long-range shot that had freed her and thrust her into the political limelight.

Chris and Mike were fiercely competitive with each other, and were always teasing each other. But above all, they were very good friends.

"I didn't hit you," Mike said, answering Chris's challenge. "If I had hit you, you would be bleeding."

"You hit my shirt, and my shirt is part of me," Chris said.

"No, your skin is part of you."

"Haven't you ever heard the expression 'You are what you wear'?"

Mike laughed. "Chris, you are as full of shit as a Christmas turkey."

"I want arbitration," Chris insisted.

"Are you bleeding?" Linda Marsh asked. Linda was sitting in a lounge chair, and she didn't look up from the book she was reading.

"No, but—"

"No buts," Linda said. "If you aren't bleeding, it's not a hit."

"Sorry, big guy. You lose," Mike said.

"Okay, now it's my time," Chris said. "Spread your legs, Mike. I'm going to see how close I can come to your balls without cutting them off."

"What?" Mike asked, putting his hands over his crotch.

Chris drew his hand back to throw, but fortunately, Wagner interrupted the play by sticking his head out the door and calling to everyone on the patio.

"Hey, guys," Wagner called. "Maybe you'd better come in here and see this."

Wagner had no field operational experience and never went on a mission, but he was the titular head of the group because he was the contact between the Code Name Team and their sponsors. He also had important contacts within the government.

"What?" Linda asked, getting up from the lounge chair.

"Harriet Clayton has just announced that she is running for President," Wagner said.

"You are calling us in to watch that?" Linda asked.

"Don taped it. Wait until you see what else she said."

The Don Wagner spoke of was Don Yee, the team's communications and computer expert.

The Code Name Team sat around the large living room making humorous and disdainful comments about the newly announced candidate until Harriet made the announcement about being rescued by the Code Name Team.

"What?" Jennifer asked in surprise, sitting up sharply. She pointed to the screen. "Did I hear right? Did that bitch just out us?"

"I'm afraid she did," Wagner replied.

"Correct me if I'm wrong, but didn't she promise to keep the whole operation confidential?" Mike asked.

"Yeah, well, so much for a politician's promises," John Barrone answered. John was the field leader of the team, the one who assigned mission responsibilities and often led the missions himself.

"What are we going to do now?" Mike asked.

"I don't know what we are going to do now, but I know what we should've done," Jennifer said.

"What's that?" Linda asked.

"Like I told John when we were in Los Angeles. We should've left her ass in the desert."

Three

Bob Crawford had been president of the Arcadia National Bank for less than two weeks, having moved his family to New Orleans from Birmingham, Alabama. He had a good position in Birmingham, but the difference in pay between his position there and his position here was significant.

When the former president of Arcadia had dropped dead of a sudden heart attack, the chairman of the board of directors for the bank, Asa Todaro, hired a headhunter to find a new president. When Bob was contacted, he accepted the offer, not only because of the increase in his personal salary, but also because of his daughter, Diane. Diane was a senior in high school, and although she had not gotten into any trouble, she had started running with what Bob considered to be a"bad" crowd.

Diane begged to be left in Birmingham long enough to graduate from school, but Bob told her that wouldn't be possible. She was having a hard time fitting in in New Orleans, partly because she wasn't trying. Bob felt bad about it, but figured that no friends at all would be better than the friends she'd had in Birmingham.

Bob saw someone drop a folder on his secretary's

desk. She thanked the man, then got up and started to put the folder in a filing cabinet. Bob got up and walked to the door of his office.

"What's that, Jean?"

"Oh, it's nothing. Just the daily transaction reports. Mr. Zarachore never wanted to see them, so I just file them."

"File them for what?"

"Oh, for a year," Jean answered. "Then they go to our retired records office downtown."

"Let me take a look at them," Bob said.

"Okay, sure. You want the whole month?"

"Yes," Bob said. "Maybe perusing the transaction reports will help me get acclimated faster."

Jean brought several file folders to him and, for the rest of the day, Bob pored over the documents. By the end of the day he'd confirmed something that he'd begun to suspect after the first few documents.

The Arcadia bank was laundering money. He didn't know who or what the ATA Corporation was, but there were few corporations, even the largest, that would have that much money passing through in so short a time. That evening, he called Asa.

"Asa, you want to drop by the bank for a few minutes? We've got a problem."

"What sort of problem?" Todaro asked.

"I'd rather not talk about it over the telephone."

The bank was closed and deserted, except for the two men in Bob's office.

"So what is the problem?" Todaro asked after Bob brought out the documents.

"Have you been tracking the daily transaction reports?" Bob asked.

Asa chuckled. "No, thanks. Looking at a bunch of figures written in little squares? That's not my job. Why do you ask?"

"Well, what do you know about ATA?"

"ATA? Good customer, solid company."

"They are laundering money," Bob said.

Todaro shook his head. "No, that can't be true. ATA has been one of our customers for almost five years now," he said. "We've gone through several audits in that time and not one hint of misconduct had come up. I can see where you might be a little suspicious, with so much money going through their account. But they are a financial operation, buying and selling companies. They deal with a lot of money. And it's very good for our bank."

"Maybe," Bob said. "Still, I would feel better if we had a bank examiner look it over and clear it."

"You don't want to do that, Bob," Todaro said. "Getting a bank examiner to come in and poke around is just asking for trouble. The truth is, the guy you replaced had a tendency to get a little sloppy from time to time. Why don't you give it another few months until you are sure that we are up to snuff in all departments? Then you can call in a bank examiner. Hell, *I'll* call one in."

"I don't know, let me think about it," Bob said. "You know, since nine-eleven, we need to be more vigilant than ever. I wouldn't want to be laundering money for terrorists."

"No," Todaro agreed. "We certainly wouldn't want to do that."

When Todaro got home that evening, his wife reminded him that Bob and Julie Crawford were coming over for dinner.

"I told them they could bring Diane too, of course," she said, "but I don't think she will be coming. Bless her heart, she is having such a difficult time adjusting to New Orleans. She's a beautiful young girl, but very troubled."

"What time are they coming?"

"About a quarter till seven, I think."

"All right. I have to run upstairs to my office to take care of a few things."

"You won't get so distracted that you forget they are coming, will you?"

"I won't forget," Todaro promised.

Once upstairs, Todaro closed the door to his office, then made a long-distance telephone call to the principal for the ATA account.

Crawford was right. The bank was being used to launder money . . . Bustamante's drug money.

"We have a problem," Todaro said when Bustamante answered.

"Don't ever call me and start your conversation with, 'We have a problem.' I am paying you very well so that we don't have problems," Bustamante replied.

"You are paying me well to keep on top of things," Todaro said. "And that's what I'm doing now. I'm telling you that we have a problem at the bank."

"What is the problem?"

Todaro explained about Crawford discovering the laundering operation.

"That is not difficult. All we need to do is get rid of him."

"No," Todaro said. "We got rid of Zarachore when he discovered what was going on. It would look pretty suspicious if another bank president suddenly had a heart attack, wouldn't it?"

"Then you had better find some way to make him change his mind."

"I don't know what that would be, unless . . ." Todaro stopped in mid-sentence. "Wait a minute. I do have an idea."

"What is your idea?"

"I think I know how to persuade him to change his mind," Todaro replied.

When Bob and Julie Crawford returned home that evening, they were surprised to find Diane gone.

"Where in the world could she be at this hour?" Bob asked.

"I don't know. And I don't feel that good about her driving around in New Orleans this late. She doesn't know the city that well," Julie said.

"Wait a minute. Her car was still in the garage, wasn't it?" Bob said. Hurrying back to the kitchen, he opened the door, then turned on the light in the three-car garage. Diane's little red Mustang was still there. He went back inside. When he did, he saw Julie standing there ashen-faced. She was holding the telephone.

"What is it? What's wrong?" Bob asked.

"I called her cell phone," Julie said. "He wants to talk to you."

"He? Who's he?" Bob asked angrily. He took the phone. "Who is this?" he demanded.

"Who I am isn't important," a man's voice said. "What is important is that we have your daughter."

"What do you mean, you have my daughter?"

"I understand you are planning to call a bank examiner to look into the ATA account. That would be a serious mistake."

"Is my daughter all right?"

"One week from now, all the money in the ATA account will be electronically transferred to another bank.

If the transfer goes through with no difficulty, we will release your daughter. If there is a glitch, you will never see your daughter again."

"Is my daughter all right?" Crawford asked, more anxiously than before.

"Hold on."

"Daddy?" Diane's voice said over the phone. "Daddy, who are these assholes who are holding me?"

"Diane, don't worry," Crawford said. "Hang on. I'll find a way to get you out of there."

"The only way you are going to get her out of here is by doing what I say," the man's voice said again. "And where did your daughter pick up such a garbage mouth? Geez, you ought to be ashamed, raising a kid that talks like that."

"If you harm one hair on her head—" Crawford began, but the kidnapper interrupted him.

"Yeah, yeah," he said. "Just remember what I said. Do nothing until the money is transferred out of your bank. Oh, and I don't have to tell you not to go to the police, do I? If I see one word of this in the papers, I'll kill this little garbage-mouthed tramp."

Hollywood, Calfornia

Shortly before the war in Iraq, movie star Nathan Alex had gone on television to announce that if the United States waged an aggressive war against another nation, he would leave the country.

"My conscience will not allow me to stand by and see one million innocent Iraqis slaughtered while we start shipping our own soldiers back in body bags by the tens of thousands," he said.

When the war was successfully fought without any of

his dire predictions coming true, he was asked on a "talking head" TV show why he didn't carry through with his threat to leave the country.

"Oh, yes," Alex replied. "The right-wing Nazis who are running our government now would like that, wouldn't they? They would like nothing better than for me to go away."

Nathan Alex looked right into the camera and, with all the skills of his profession, spoke directly to the nation of viewers.

"But I promise you, the people of America, that I will not go away. I will stay right here and throw my support behind those candidates who are willing to take the bold steps necessary to stop this nation's insidious slide to the right."

This time Nathan Alex was true to his word. When Senator Harriet Clayton used the notoriety of her narrow escape from terrorists in the desert of Sitarkistan to announce her candidacy for President of the United States, the movie actor was the first person to host a gala fund-raising event.

Outside Rose Hill, Alex's Beverly Hills mansion, off-duty policemen were hired to turn away the curious, and allow entry only to those who could present an invitation. In the warm, almost tropical climate of southern California, the Christmas decorations seemed somewhat incongruous, but the private guards were part of it, wearing gala little bells with red and green ribbons just above their badges.

The house and grounds were also decorated for the Christmas season, and filled with the "beautiful" people of Hollywood. But beyond the greenery and tinsel, there was none of the Christmas spirit. These were people who, for too long now, had enjoyed little sway with the

White House, and they were showing their frustration by the animus of the signs that were posted about the estate. The signs were everywhere, reading PEACE NOW, NO BLOOD FOR OIL, and AMERICA MUST APOLOGIZE.

There were also large caricatures of American soldiers, wearing WWII German-style helmets, complete with swastikas. The cartoons depicted the American GIs with blood-dripping bayonets, wading through slaughtered burka-clad women and dismembered Arab children.

Along with the peace signs were several that read LEGAL-IZE DRUGS, and working the crowd were the connections of some of the elite users.

"It is pejorative and demeaning to use the term addicts," a spokesman for the ACLU had said in a recent interview. *"The term of choice is 'user,' which indicates that an adult has made a mature choice for his or her own life."*

A rap band was performing out by the swimming pool. Dressed in lamé and covered with gold chains and body-piercings, the lead singer's black skin glistened with sweat as he gyrated to the words he had written just for this occasion:

> *It's time to bring the muthas down*
> *They ain' wearin' no fuckin' crown*
> *Washington be the people's town*
> *Don't need no mo assholes aroun'*
> *Goin' to take a gun and clean up the place*
> *Cain't be scared off by no Whitey's mace*
> *Goin' to bash the muthas right in the face*
> *Build us a world ain't got no race*
> *Where the sistas all put out*
> *Come on let's hear a shout*
> *For the revolution don't you know*
> *That's goin' take down all you mo fo*
> *Goin' to move in class*

Goin' to get some ass
Goin' to get some ass
Goin' to get some ass.

The actual words were nearly lost in the rhythm of the drums and the slurring mouthing of the lyrics. That made no difference to the people who were gathered around the pool, because they cheered and gyrated with the easy assurance of someone who was certain that, whatever the words were, it was chic and politically correct to show appreciation.

Just inside the house, in the large foyer, a chamber orchestra played softer, more soothing music and the older attendees, in tuxedos and high-fashion gowns, stood in little groups, drinking martinis and lamenting the fact that cable TV had so diluted the power of the once-powerful anchors of the network evening news programs.

Two young actors, who really had no interest at all in politics, but had come to the party because it was the most happening thing in Hollywood, took their recently purchased cocaine and started through the house, looking for a private place to do a line. Going upstairs, they walked down a long hallway until they saw a door that they were sure led to an out-of-the-way bathroom.

"In here," one of them said, pushing open the door.

Just inside, with her dress hiked up and her bare bottom resting on a lavatory, was Suzann Strawn, Nathan Alex's wife and a famous actress in her own right. Her bare legs were spread and wrapped around the waist of one of the hired waiters, who was pumping away.

"Do you mind?" Suzann asked in an irritated but not alarmed voice. "If you two little boys want to diddle each other, find your own place. This one is taken."

From outside came the sound of sirens, then a rising crescendo of cheers and applause.

"Sounds like the bitch has just arrived," Suzann said.

"I'd better go," the waiter said.

"Honey, if you leave before I'm finished, I'll cut your balls off," Suzann said, reaching down to grab him. She looked up at the two young actors, who had been shocked into immobility by what they had tumbled into.

"If you're going to stay and watch, stay. If you're going to leave, leave," she said. "Either way, shut the damn door."

Harriet Clayton, former Second Lady of the nation, had, even as her husband was running for President, taken up residence in the state of New Jersey in order to run for Senator. While her husband's candidacy was unsuccessful, Harriet succeeded, and she was now New Jersey's junior Senator.

Her successful campaign had propelled her to a position of prominence within the national party, though there were many in the state party who resented her interloper status. There were some within her own party in the state who were quietly making plans to dump her during the next election. All that had changed, though, when Harriet went to Sitarkistan to meet personally with Abdul Kadan Kadar, a terrorist who had launched a series of attacks against the United States.

Sitarkistan, one year earlier

Kadar agreed to meet with her, allowing her to bring the television journalist Douglas Sharbell with her, but insisting that their meeting be kept secret from any official of the U.S. Government until after she had returned. Harriet agreed to the terms, swearing her staff to secrecy, and not even telling her husband what she had in mind. Kadar had gone to great lengths to keep the meeting a secret, and Harriet was convinced that not even those people she had met at the various stops along the way knew anything beyond their own little pieces of information. It wasn't that they were being incommunicative when she asked them questions; it was just that they didn't know the answers.

Harriet remembered reading once about the French Underground. It seemed that they all had worked in the same disconnected way during World War II. There were cells who would transport downed Allied pilots back to safety, never knowing where the pilots came from, nor where they would go after the cells were through with them. It didn't take much for Harriet to imagine that she was like one of those downed pilots now.

Despite the inconvenience and discomfort she had experienced during this trip, and the gravity of the mission, Harriet felt a slight thrill at being a part of this clandestine movement.

Douglas Sharbell, Harriet's companion on the trip, was a left-leaning television journalist whose anti-government commentaries had bought him entrée with the terrorists. It was actually Sharbell's connections with the terrorists that had enabled Harriet to make the connections she needed for the meeting. Shortly after Harriet and Sharbell met with Kadar, Sharbell began taping an exclusive.

"I am Douglas Sharbell," the journalist began. "The United States Government would pay twenty-five million dollars to anyone who can do what I am about to do. I am in a secret location" —he looked around— "so secret that I don't even know where it is. Even though I can't tell you where I am, I can tell you that this is the camp, the headquarters if you will, of Abdul Kadan Kadar. That's right, ladies and gentlemen, I am about to bring you an exclusive interview with the most sought-after man in the world, Abdul Kadan Kadar."

As Sharbell continued his introuction, an arm came into the picture. The arm was behind Sharbell, and Sharbell, who was speaking into the camera, saw neither the arm nor the curved knife that was in the hand.

Shockingly, the knife made a quick slashing motion across the front of Sharbell's neck, and blood began gushing forth like a fountain. The expression on Sharbell's face turned from one of arrogant achievement, to surprise, to horror, all in less than a second. Then, even as he fell, his eyes were rolling back into his head.

Kadar then took the microphone and spoke into the camera.

"To the government of the American people, let this serve as a warning to you. Senator Clayton is now our prisoner. If our demands are not met, what you have just seen happen to America's most popular journalist will happen to her, and to any American who sets foot anywhere on our holy ground, not just in Sitarkistan, but in all Muslim countries. You will not be safe, even in those countries you consider your friends. We will kill all Americans, and if you send your soldiers after us, we will kill them too."

Senator Clayton was ultimately rescued by the Code Name Team. Her interference compromised an ongoing U.S. mission, but despite that, the fact that she had been in such high-profile danger had sent her political stock soaring.

Hollywood, Califorian, the present

As the stretch limousine bearing Harriet arrived, she smiled and waved through the window at the enthusiastic greeting of the Hollywood crowd. With bobbed blond hair and big blue eyes, she was just short of being pretty, and had it not been for her power and wealth, might even be considered frumpy.

"Look at all these pampered assholes," Harriet said, speaking without moving her lips so that the big smile remained.

"My dear," Henry Norton said. "These 'pampered assholes' have provided you with nearly five million dollars so far. And if you get your party's nomination, you can count on them for another five. Be charming. They have paid for it."

"Isn't it enough that I am smart and the best candidate?" Harriet asked. "Do I have to be charming too?"

"I'm afraid so, my dear. I'm afraid so."

Secret Service agents exited her car, as well as the one following. Looking over the crowd and the grounds with trained eyes, the Secret Service guards called their clearances into wrist-mounted microphones.

"Man at the corner of the pool is holding something in his hand," one of the agents said.

"It's all right, I have a good visual. He's a gardener, that's a trowel."

"All clear here."

"Clear."

Senator Clayton now had twelve years of experience with personal bodyguards, and they had become as invisible to her as potted plants. She never spoke to them, smiled at them, or thanked them, and even now, as they made certain her arrival was safe, she started toward Nathan Alex with her hand extended and a huge smile plastered on her face.

"Nathan," she said gushingly. "How wonderful of you to host this fund-raiser."

"Anything for our next President," Nathan said.

"From your mouth to God's ear," Harriet replied.

"Come, let me introduce you to a few people who might be able to do you some good."

"Why, it's as if every star in Hollywood has turned out for this event," Harriet said. "I'm awestruck. Absolutely awestruck."

"They are all friends of mine," Nathan said. "Just ordinary Americans, like everyone else. And as concerned with America's future as is everyone else."

"Hardly ordinary," Harriet retorted.

"Well, as ordinary as any other American who makes several million dollars per picture and whose name is instantly recognized all over the country," Nathan said with a self-deprecating laugh.

Harriet followed Nathan into the grand foyer of his home, a huge entry hall that was itself nearly twice the size of the average American home. An orchestra was playing and, at a cue from Nathan, they played "Ruffles and Flourishes," followed by "Hail to the Chief."

Laughing, Harriet held her hands up and shook her head to stop the music.

"Thank you," she said. "I'm flattered . . . truly flattered. But by law, that music is only to be played at the entrance of the President."

"The band was just practicing for the next time you pay us a visit," Nathan said. "And if the current occupant of the White House doesn't like it, well, then let that warmongering son of a bitch come arrest me," he added.

"Yes, and me too," the bandleader said.

"You are too kind," Harriet said. "And I must say that I can't find fault, either with your choice of music, or with your assessment of the President."

The guests, who were gathering nearer now, laughed.

"Senator, what is your take on the war?"

"War?" Harriet replied. "Surely you aren't referring to the situation of several hundred thousand men running around in the desert and in the mountains as war, are you? Because if you are, let me remind you that there was a time when our nation fought wars only when it was in our vital interest to do so. World War I was such a war. World War II was another just war. We began to stray off course with the Korean War, and got drastically off course during the Vietnam War. Fortunately, it was then that the American public recognized the futility of war, and most intelligent people came to the belief that never again would our nation get involved in a war that served no legitimate purpose."

"You say that, Senator, but here we are, fighting another war that nobody supports."

"Yes, I'm afraid that is true," Harriet said. "That's the bad news." She smiled broadly. "But the good news is there is a way to turn this all around. There is a way to stop the war and bring all of our men and women home. And you all know what that way is."

"Harriet Clayton for President!" Nathan shouted, and nearly all the others repeated his shout, followed by several hurrahs.

There was one actor, however, who did not join the others in their vocal support for Harriet. Gil Lasher had made a name for himself in action movies, often playing American heroes. He was a man who believed in the qualities of the men he portrayed.

"You would bring our troops home, would you, Senator Clayton?" he asked.

"Absolutely," Harriet insisted.

"Then what?"

"What do you mean, then what? I don't understand your question."

"Do you think if we picked up all our marbles and went home, that the terrorists who struck us on nine-eleven would quit?"

"I believe that, yes."

"You mean you would leave the field to the enemy, just as we did in Beirut, and just as we did in Somalia?"

"Something like that, yes."

"Don't you think that there is a possibility that nine-eleven happened precisely because we left Beirut and Somalia?"

"Boo!" some of the others shouted. "What are you, some right-wing nut?"

"Gil, don't tell me you are beginning to take to heart some of those hokey pictures you make," someone shouted.

"I don't regard them as hokey," Gil said. "On the contrary, I regard them as pictures with moral value, pictures that are honest, patriotic, and honorable."

"Someone run a flag up a pole so ole Gil can salute it," somebody shouted.

"Better yet, run a flagpole up that old fool's ass and *we'll* salute him," another called out, and his slur was met with a round of laughter, including laughter from Harriet Clayton.

"He doesn't need a flag to be saluted," one of Harriet's Secret Service guards said, in a breach of silence that was very rare for an official bodyguard. "Mr. Lasher, I was in the military during Operation Desert Storm when you came to visit the troops. My father was in Vietnam when you visited the troops there." The bodyguard came to attention and saluted. "I thank you, sir."

"No, sir, I and all Americans thank you," the actor replied.

"Maybe you two want to be alone so you can kiss," one of Nathan's guests said.

"What? Gil Lasher is gay? What will his right-wing fans say when they find that out?" Nathan asked, and again, the crowd convulsed in laughter.

"Get that Secret Service man on the next plane back to Washington," Harriet said quietly to Henry Norton.

"But Senator, he is chief of the guard detail," Norton replied in shock.

"He is too right-wing for me."

"He may be a little conservative, but I assure you, whether he agrees with your politics or not, he would take a bullet for you."

"I want him out of here," Harriet said again, more insistent this time.

"All right. I think you are making a mistake, but I'll take care of it," Norton said.

"See that you do," Harriet replied. Then, smiling and extending her hand, she greeted Suzann Strawn, who was just arriving on the scene looking flushed and strangely bemused.

"Suzann, how nice to see you," Harriet said.

Suzann took Harriet's extended hand. "I must apologize for not being here to meet you, I was . . . uh . . . in the middle of something that I just had to finish," she said. "I do hope you understand."

Harriet was where she was in her political career because she missed very little. She had seen Suzann and a young waiter come into the foyer together, and she had seen the look the two exchanged just before they separated.

"Oh, but I do understand," Harriet said pointedly. "Believe me. I understand far better than you realize." Her eyes cut toward the young waiter, who was just now picking up a tray of drinks and explaining to the head waiter why he'd been detained.

Suzann saw the direction of Harriet's glance, but instead of being embarrassed, she was amused. A sly smile played across her lips.

"You know, I think you do understand at that," she

said. "Has Nathan introduced you to our guests? Come with me."

"It's a little too late to . . . come . . . with you, isn't it?" Harriet replied.

"What?" Suzann asked in surprise.

"Nathan has already introduced me."

"Oh!" Suzann replied. "Oh! I thought . . . I thought you were referring to something else."

"Yes, well, from the looks of things, it's too late for that as well, I believe," Harriet said.

Suzann laughed out loud. "Senator Clayton," she said. You are a sharp and 'with it' broad. You are going to make one hell of a President."

"Why, I thank you, Suzann," Harriet replied graciously.

Four

The painted sign on the back of the shrimp boat identified it as *Lucille,* out of Bayou LaBatre, Alabama. It was anchored just off Grand Grosier Island, Louisiana. With its sweeps, cranes, and tackle extended, the forty-five-foot blue-and-white trawler looked very much like a schooner under sail.

John Barrone stood on deck, looking toward the island through a pair of binoculars. In his early fifties, John was six feet two inches tall, with blue eyes and gray hair. Like everyone else on the team, John had spent a long career with the government, in his case, twenty-two years with the CIA.

John's wife, Michelle, had been dead for nearly ten years now, and there had been no serious romances in his life since then. He did keep an eight-by-ten framed picture of her by his bed, though, and on those nights when he managed to sleep in his own bed (there weren't that many), he told her good night.

"See anything?" Jennifer Barnes asked.

"Yeah," John said. "There's a house on stilts at the north end of the island. "Wait a minute. Someone just came out onto the porch." He made a slight adjustment to the glasses. "He's armed. He's carrying an AK-47."

"What are the chances that some coon-ass will be walking around carrying an AK-47? Carrying a rifle or a shotgun maybe, but not an AK-47. This has to be the place," Jennifer said.

"Yeah, I think this is it," John said.

Chris Farmer and Mike Rojas came on deck then.

"What've we got?" Chris asked.

"Somebody walking around on the porch of that house, carrying an AK-47," Jennifer said.

"Any sign of the girl?" Mike asked.

John shook his head. "Nothing."

"We're going in anyway, aren't we?"

"You damn right we are," John answered. "As soon as it gets dark."

John and the Code Name Team were on a special assignment to rescue Diane Crawford.

After talking to the kidnapper on his daughter's cell phone, and being frightened away from going to the police, Bob called his brother-in-law in New York to get his advice. Julie's brother, Dan Heckemeyer, was a high-powered lawyer, and a friend of Bob's even before Bob married his sister.

Heckemeyer represented a man named Marist J. Quinncannon. Quinncannon was a very wealthy man who had used the services of a group of freelance law enforcers known as the Code Name Team to seek revenge for the murder of his granddaughter.*

"If I were you, I would go to the Code Name Team," Heckemeyer said.

"The Code Name Team? I've never heard of them. Who are they?"

"They are the elite of the elite," the lawyer replied.

"But what can they do?"

---

* *Code Name Death*

"What can they do? If Diane is still alive, they can get her back for you. That's what they can do."

Through his connection with Quinncannon, Heckemeyer managed to put Bob in touch with the Code Name Team. Bob explained the situation, and the Code Name Team agreed to take the case.

Don had Bob call his daughter's cell phone a few times, ostensibly to inquire on Diane's condition and to assure the kidnappers that he had gone to neither the bank examiner nor the law.

With the phone calls, Don managed to get a fix on the tower that was transmitting the signal from Diane's phone, thus enabling him to pinpoint their position.

"They are right here," Don said, pointing to a little island on the map. *"Grand Grosier Island."*

"They can't be," Bob said. *"According to the map, there's nobody there. It's all marsh."*

"Can you think of a better place to hide than a deserted island?" John asked.

It was late afternoon now, and the sun went down with a brilliant display of color. To the casual observer, the scene displayed was a bright and shining picture, a beautiful print, suitable for framing.

Although the boat added to the romance of the scene, it was not as it appeared. Instead of a tranquil fishing trawler working the Gulf banks, it was a staging platform for a quasi-military operation, an electronic eavesdropper loaded with radio and surveillance equipment.

John, Jennifer, Chris, and Mike were dressed all in black, and as the sun went down, they began to smear camouflage paint on their faces and exposed skin. All four had belts that fairly bristled with equipment, to include pistols and knives.

"Don?" John called.

Don Yee stuck his head out of the boat cabin. As usual he was eating, at the moment a jellied doughnut.

"Yeah?"

"Anything new?"

"One of them just called his girlfriend back in New Orleans," Don said. "Their conversation got pretty graphic. Want the details?"

John chuckled. "No, thanks. What about Diane?"

"She must be a spitfire," Don said. "There have been three calls complaining about how hard she is to handle."

"But she's still alive?"

"I think so. The last call that mentioned her was about four this afternoon, and from the tone of the conversation, she was alive then."

"Good," John said. He looked toward the others. "Is everyone ready?"

He received affirmative nods all the way around.

"All right, into the boat," he ordered.

The four walked to the side of the trawler that was away from the island, then slipped over the edge and climbed down into a rubber raft. It was dark and, with the quiet hum of an electric motor, the little raft started the three-mile run into shore.

"Watch your footing once we get there," John warned. "There's very little solid ground."

"Yeah, and what solid ground there is will be crawling with snakes," Chris added.

"Snakes?" Mike asked in alarm.

Chris knew that there was really very little chance that any snakes would be on the marshy island, but he knew Mike's aversion to them, and was just having a little fun.

"Ah, don't worry about it, Mike. There are only four kinds of poisonous snakes in America: rattlesnakes, coral, copperhead, and cottonmouth," Chris said.

"Which kind do they have here?" Mike asked.

"Oh, I think they have all four," Chris said, laughing.

"Shh," John cautioned. "We're getting close now, and sound carries across water."

Not another word was spoken as the little rubber raft cut through the surf, then slipped up into one of the bayous. John found a bit of solid ground and they landed there, then left the raft.

"What kind of security?" Jennifer asked.

"We think they have at least six guards," John said. "And as small as the house is, there will be someone with the girl all the time."

Inside the house

Diane Crawford was seventeen years old, and if the kidnappers had thought fear would keep her docile, they had another think coming. She fought them tooth and nail from the moment they captured her, biting and scratching until they finally managed to get her tied up. Now, as they waited for the next move, Diane was tied to a wooden kitchen chair.

"Hey, Pig-face," Diane said to one of her captors. "I've got to pee."

"Just hold it for a while," the one she called Pig-face replied.

"I can't hold it. Come on, you've got a bathroom in here. What's the harm in letting me use it?"

"Because the last time you used it, you tried to crawl out through the window," Pig-face replied.

"Well, yeah, but I didn't get away."

"I know you didn't. I caught you."

"Yes, you are just too smart for me," Diane said.

"You damn right I am. I've dealt with your kind before," Pig-face said.

"So, what will it take to get you to let me go to the bathroom?" Diane asked. "Oh, I know. You want to watch me pee? Do you get off by watching young girls pee? How about if you squat down and I pee on you? Would you like that?"

"Geez, you have a filthy mouth," Pig-face said. "If I'd'a talked like that when I was your age, my ole man would've washed my mouth out with soap."

"Will you for chrissake quit arguing with her?" one of the others asked.

"Come on, Arnie, you've heard her mouthing off the way she has. I mean, tell her to shut up or somethin'."

"She's just trying to get your goat," Arnie said.

As Pig-face looked at Diane, he repeatedly slid open and shut the bolt on his AK-47, though only partially so, not enough to eject a shell.

"Will you stop playing with your gun like that?" Arnie said. "What the fuck are you doing?"

"I know what he's doing," Diane said. "I took a college course in psychology. He's jerking off with that gun."

Arnie and the other captors laughed.

"I'll show you jerking off," Pig-face said, pulling his hand back to slap her.

"Hold it!" Arnie called. "Our orders are nobody is to touch her until we get the word."

"Yeah?" Pig-face replied. "Well, when we get the word to off this bitch, I want to be the one to do it."

"When we get the word, if you want her, you can have her. It's sure no sweat off my balls."

Pig-face looked at Diane and smiled evilly. "I'm going to enjoy killing you. The only thing is, I don't know if I want to cut out your heart, or blow your head off," he said. "Either way, I'm going to enjoy it."

Diane was not nearly as brave as she had been letting on. Her bravado was merely her means of keeping herself from completely breaking down, but with Pig-face's cold, calm assertion that he was going to kill her, her bravado abandoned her for a moment and the fear showed in her eyes.

Pig-face saw the momentary panic, and his evil smile broadened. "Well, you aren't quite as tough as you thought you were, are you, bitch?" he asked.

At that exact moment there was a loud explosion outside, followed by a long burst of machine-gun fire.

Three of the captors burst into the room.

"The law is here!" one of them shouted.

The gunfire was close, loud, very fierce, coming up through the swamp and moving closer. All the kidnappers in the room except for Pig-face raced outside with their weapons.

"Diane Crawford!" someone shouted. "Diane, if you can hear me, tell us where you are!"

"I'm in here!" Diane called. "I'm in the house!"

Running to one of the windows, Pig-face squeezed off a short burst of automatic fire. Then, before Diane's shocked and horrified eyes, she saw blood and brain matter spew from the back of Pig-face's head, like lava from an erupting volcano. He fell back onto the floor, spewing blood onto her pants legs.

Almost immediately thereafter, John kicked in the front door and raced into the house. Outside, gunfire continued.

John cut her loose from the chair. "Get down," he shouted, making a motion with his hand. "Get down on the floor!"

Diane did as she was ordered.

John ran to the window and looked outside, but he didn't see a target.

"John, we're secure!" Mike Rojas shouted, bursting

into the house then. "Five . . ." Looking toward Pig-face's body, he amended the report. "Six bad guys down."

"Let's get her out of here, and back to her father," John suggested. "Remember, we aren't operating on any governmental authority."

"Right," Mike agreed. "Let's go."

As he, Diane, and Mike ran down the steps, John saw the bodies of the other kidnappers. One was on the porch at the top of the stairs; four more were on the ground below. Chris and Jennifer were at the foot of the stairs, their weapons at the ready.

"Everyone all right?" John called.

"We're fine," Jennifer answered. "How about the girl?"

"She's fine," John replied.

"No, I'm not," Diane said in a weak voice.

John looked around in surprise. "Were you hit?" he asked. "Where were you hit? Do you need attention?"

"I wasn't hit," Diane said. "But I wet my pants."

Five

New Orleans

With his daughter safely back home, Bob Crawford called the bank examiner to tell him what he found. The bank examiner backed up Crawford's finding of a laundering operation and the account was seized.

For Pablo Bustamante, the seizure of the account couldn't have come at a worse time. Christmas was approaching, and always during the holiday season, the demand on the street went up. He needed product to meet that demand, and he needed the money that was in his account to pay for a new shipment.

To this end, he had arranged for three of his Colombian suppliers to meet with him in New Orleans. He met them in a fifteen-hundred-dollar-per-night suite in a New Orleans hotel.

"Have some caviar," Bustamante invited.

"I don't like caviar," one of the three said.

"To be sure, it's an acquired taste," Bustamante said as he used a silver spoon to scoop some onto a cracker. "But it is a taste worth acquiring."

"You have the money?" one of the others asked.

"Do you mean with me? No, I don't have it with me. Do you have my product with you?"

"No."

"No, of course not. I called this meeting to discuss our, uh, arrangements."

"Nothing to discuss. You give us money, we give you product. You know what our price is."

"Yes, well, about the money. There may be a little difficulty there."

"What sort of difficulty? Do you have the money or not?"

Bustamante chuckled. "Of course I have the money. I have more money than God," he said.

"Then there is no problem."

"Well, yes, unfortunately there is a problem," Bustamante replied. "I don't have it in an accessible account."

"What does that mean?"

"My accessible account has been seized by the feds. Money laundering."

"Get more."

"You don't understand the problem. It is extremely difficult to move large sums of money around in U.S. banks now, especially since nine-eleven. If I used an unlaundered account to buy the next shipment from you, the feds would be on me like stink on shit."

"So, what are you asking?"

"I'm asking you to give me some time to get a new laundry in place."

"All right, take the time."

Bustamante smiled. "Good, good. I knew you would understand."

"As soon as you have money you can spend, contact us. We'll supply you with more product."

"What? No, you don't understand," Bustamante said. "I need it now! I've got a network that has to be supplied. If I don't supply them, they will go somewhere else."

"It makes no difference to us," the spokesman said. "If you don't buy from us, someone else will."

"But I have been your best customer."

"And we appreciate that. Contact us again when you have money."

Bustamante watched with a sickening, sinking feeling in his stomach as the three Colombians left. Shortly after they left, he called Asa Todaro, his man in New Orleans, and asked him to come to the hotel to meet with him.

"Who are these incompetent bastards you hired?" Bustamante asked angrily. "You told me they could handle the job."

"They were good men," Todaro said. "I was told they were the best New Orleans had to offer."

"The best, huh? Well, all I can say is, the best New Orleans had to offer were as worthless as shit. It's a good thing for them they are dead. Because if they weren't, I'd kill the bastards myself."

"Who would've thought the Code Name Team would get involved in something like this?"

"The Code Name Team. You are talking about the people who rescued her?" He picked up the *Times-Picayune* and read from the story. "'My rescuers were as heroic as any movie I've ever seen,' Diane Crawford said. 'Three men and a woman came out of the night, dressed like ninjas. . . .'" Bustamante looked up from the article. "Dressed like ninjas? What the hell is that all about? Who dresses like ninjas? DEA, FBI, Louisiana State Police, the parish sheriff's department? Who the hell are these ninjas?" Bustamante slapped the paper with the back of his hand.

"I told you, they are the Code Name Team."

"The Code Name Team? Wait a minute. Aren't they the assholes who butted into my trial out in California?"

"Yes."

"Well, hell, that turned out just fine. In fact, I meant

to send them a thank-you card for taking an interest in me," Bustamante said with a chuckle.

Todaro shook his head. "They aren't the kind of people you want to have take an interest in you. They are some bad asses."

"Bad asses, huh? Well, I can raise a few bad asses of my own."

"You want me to try and find out more about them?" Todaro asked.

Bustamante slapped the rolled-up paper against the palm of his hand a few times. "No," he said. "Not right now. Right now it looks like our friends in Colombia aren't going to be very cooperative, so I've got to find some other way to stay in business. And I've got to do it fast."

El Desemboque, Mexico

The small village of El Desemboque was the perfect location for Bustamante's drug factory. If his Colombian suppliers weren't going to work with him, then to hell with them. He would bring in his own raw material, build his own factory, and be totally self-sufficient.

Bustamante and his business manager, Baldwin Carter, met with Jose Mendoza at the little Seri Indian village on the Sea of Cortez in Sonora, Mexico. Bustamante had considered flying down, but there was no landing strip for an airplane, and a helicopter would call too much attention to them. On the other hand, Mendoza pointed out, Desemboque was a port of call for fishing yachts from the U.S., so one more boat wouldn't cause anyone to take a second look.

They anchored the boat just off the coast, then came ashore in a small speedboat. As they met over margueritas at an outside café, there was music and dancing going on in the street behind them.

"It is the Desert Pilgrimage," Mendoza explained. "Every year the Seri, Tohono, and Yaqui people walk two hundred miles through the desert."

"Why the hell would they do that?" Bustamante asked.

"An old custom of an ignorant people," Mendoza answered with a dismissive wave of his hand. "Do you have the money, Señor?"

"Yes. One million dollars in cash," Bustamante said. He nodded at Baldwin, who after glancing around to make certain that no one was watching, opened the briefcase he was carrying. The briefcase was filled with stacks of one-hundred-dollar bills.

"I will trust you that it is all there," Mendoza said, and Baldwin closed the case.

"That is a lot of money, Mendoza."

"It takes a lot of money to build the kind of operation you want. I have to start everything from scratch. The land must be bought, the machinery brought in, the workers hired, the security arranged. And, of course, there are the payoffs, the money we must pay the officials in order to be able to work."

"Don't disappoint me."

"I will not, Señor. But," Mendoza said, holding up his hand, "I must have the raw material to work with. And all local supply is tied up by the Medellin."

"I have found a new source of supply," Bustamante said.

"Dependable?"

"Many times more dependable than the Medellin. You don't worry about that. All you worry about is having this plant up, and online, by the time I bring you the first shipment. Have you found a place for the factory yet?"

Mendoza smiled. "*Sí*. It is on the Isla del Angel Guardión," he said. "The Island of the Guardian Angel."

"Why there?"

"There are no villages on the island. Also no roads and no airport. The only way there is by boat. It will be very secure."

"What about workers?"

"You let me worry about that, Señor," Mendoza said. "We will have all the workers we need."

"And the police?"

"Will visit the island only if we invite them," Mendoza insisted.

"Good, good. That sounds very good."

Mendoza looked over at Baldwin Carter, who was a very obvious American, then turned back to Bustamante.

"*He organizado a mujeres para el placer para usted. Pero, tal vez este hombre prefiere a hombres?*"

Mendoza lifted his hand, and two beautiful women and an effeminate-looking young man stood up from a nearby table, awaiting an invitation to join them.

Bustamante laughed. "Thank you, no," he said. "We must be getting back."

Mendoza dismissed them with a second wave, and with looks of disappointment, they returned to their table. "You'll be hearing from me," Bustamante said, reaching across the table to shake Mendoza's hand.

Hanging on to the briefcase full of money, Mendoza didn't rise as Bustamante and Baldwin waked back down to the beach for the boat ride back to their yacht.

"What did he say?" Baldwin asked.

"You heard him. He's going to get the factory assembled for us."

"No, I mean when he spoke in Spanish. What did he say?"

"He said that he had arranged some women for our pleasure," Bustamante said.

"I saw the women. They were beautiful. Who was the man with them?"

Bustamante laughed. "Jose Mendoza is a man who likes to please," he said. "The man was for you."

Zabakabad, Sitarkistan

Mohammed Jahmshidi Mehdi hailed a cab in front of the Sharik Hotel. The yellow Mercedes left the stream of traffic and stopped at the curb.

"Zabakabad International Airport," Jahmshidi said as he slid into the backseat.

The driver nodded, but said nothing as he pulled back into the traffic.

Jahmshidi clutched the briefcase close to his chest. Inside the briefcase were plans for the next phase of the war against the American infidels.

Jahmshidi allowed a small smile of satisfaction to play across his lips as he considered the beautiful irony of it all. The Americans had sent an army into Afghanistan to destroy the Taliban and El Quaeda groups. They had been successful in that the Taliban no longer controlled Afghanistan and El Quaeda had been sent into hiding. The U.S. Government had followed the Afghanistan operation with a triumphant invasion of Iraq, where they had deposed Saddam Hussein and rooted out the Baath Party.

The Americans had displayed their amazing weapons and awesome firepower for the rest of the world to see. They were unstoppable, or so it would seem. But Jahmshidi believed he had come up with a plan to stop them. He would destroy the United States by turning the infidels' sinful behavior against itself.

Few recognized his name now, but surely, after the success of this operation, the name Mohammed Jahmshidi Mehdi would become one that faithful Muslims the world over would revere. Now, everyone knew Osama Bin Laden, and Saddam Hussein, but only the most knowledgeable intelligence operators knew the name Jahmshidi Mehdi. That would all change, though, when Jahmshidi put his plan into operation.

The fields of the Middle East were fertile growing grounds for the poppy that was necessary to make heroin. The milk from the poppy was coveted by the drug lords in South America, and for several years now, the Islamic terrorists had supplied the raw material in exchange for the money needed to fund their homicidal attacks.

But Jahmshidi Mehdi was about to take the process to the next step. Today he would meet with Pablo Bustamante, one of the most powerful drug lords in America. The purpose of the meeting was to discuss a new arrangement. Instead of selling the raw material to Bustamante, Jahmshidi Mehdi was going to propose that he provide an unlimited amount of raw material. In return for this unlimited supply, Bustamante would conduct terrorist activities against Americans.

It would be an unholy alliance. Jahmshidi was well aware that the Muslim religion preached against drugs, and believed that anyone who used or dealt in drugs was committing a grave sin. But Jahmshidi also believed that in the battle against the infidel Americans, it was sometimes necessary, and forgivable, to make a pact with the devil, if it served the greater purpose of Islam.

The tiny Kingdom of Sitarkistan was an ideal operating base for Jahmshidi, who was actually born in Saudi Arabia. Sitarkistan had no oil, so the only thing the royal family had to sell was their national sovereignty. They had no extradition treaties with any other country; therefore, international criminals could find safe haven within their borders. International fugitives paid handsomely for this welcome.

It was in just such a way that Jahmshidi had first made contact with Pablo Bustamante, for not only were international thieves and murderers granted sanctuary, so were terrorists and drug lords.

"No, not the main terminal," Jahmshidi said as the driver started in that direction. "Down there, at the far end of the field."

Again, the driver nodded without comment and drove in the direction Jahmshidi indicated.

At the far end of the tarmac sat a 727. The airplane was all white, except for the broad gold band that ran the length of the fuselage at the window level. This was Bustamante's private plane.

The tail ramp was lowered as the taxi approached the plane.

"This will do," Jahmshidi said, leaning over the seat to pay his fare.

The driver, as uncommunicative as ever, took the money. As soon as Jahmshidi stepped out of the cab, the driver pulled away.

Bustamante himself came down the tail ramp to greet Jahmshidi.

"Jahmshidi, my friend," he said, smiling broadly. "It is good to see you."

Jahmshidi nodded.

"Come aboard," Bustamante offered. "I have arranged for a little entertainment."

"I have not come to be entertained," Jahmshidi said. "I have come as a warrior for Islam."

"I understand," Bustamante said.

Jahmshidi followed Bustamante up the steps and into the airplane.

"Oh!" he gasped as he looked around. The after-cabin of the airplane looked like something from the *Tales of Arabian Nights*. At least half a dozen incredibly beautiful women, all dressed in the most diaphanous clothing imaginable, lay on silken pillows.

"There aren't seventy-two of them. And none of them are virgins. But it's a little sample of what it might be like when you reach paradise, eh, my friend?" Bustamante said. He held his hand out toward the women and motioned for three of them to come forward.

Smiling seductively, the three women stepped up to Jahmshidi. The smell of their perfume maddened his senses, and his head reeled. One of the women leaned forward and blew her sweet breath into his ear. The other two women reached down to fondle him, both their hands coming together at the place where he was most sensitive.

"But of course, if none of this is for you, I will respect your wishes," Bustamante said. A dismissive wave of his hand sent the three women back to the silk pillows.

"Uh, no," Jahmshidi said breathlessly. "You've gone to all this trouble. It would be impolite for me to refuse your offer of hospitality."

Six

Baldwin was thirty-five years old, thin and balding. He slid his glasses back up his nose as he arranged flowers in the cobalt-blue Ming dynasty vase. The vase, like everything else, belonged to Baldwin's employer, Pablo Bustamante.

The house was sixty thousand square feet, though as it was constructed to take advantage of the rocks and hills, nobody driving by on the road would suspect that it was anywhere near that large. Pablo Bustamante had planned it that way. He wanted the luxury and room of a very large and elegant house, but he wanted to do it in a way that would not attract unwanted attention.

Fortunately for him, Fountain Hills was filled with multimillion-dollar homes, each one trying to outdo the others for opulence and elegance. Because of that, Bustamante's house, understated as it was, faded into the background. Few who drove by realized that they were passing the home of one of the wealthiest drug lords in the world. Had Bustamante been able to publicize his income and net worth, he would be listed as one of the wealthiest men in America.

"Isn't Pablo coming back today?" a female voice asked. Turning, Baldwin saw Amber D'Amour, a beautiful former model, the latest in a string of beautiful women who decorated the house. He saw also that she was high.

"Yes, Miss D'Amour," Baldwin said.

Smiling, Amber walked over to him, sucked on her finger, then put it on his lip. "Is it true, Baldwin, that you like only boys?"

"I don't care to discuss my personal life with you, Miss D'Amour."

"We have time to have a little fun before Pablo returns."

"Fun?"

"Yeah, fun," Amber said, reaching down to grab his crotch. "Pablo says you like only boys. But I think I can change your mind."

"I think not," Baldwin said, moving away from her.

"Why not?" Amber asked, arching one hip out lustily, proudly. "You aren't afraid of big, bad Pablo, are you?"

"I would be afraid if I did something like that, yes," Baldwin said. "But I have no intention of doing anything like that."

"You don't like me very much, do you, Baldwin?" Amber asked, pouting.

"I neither like nor dislike you," Baldwin said. "You are a beautiful addition to the house. Like a lovely vase."

"Like a lovely vase," Amber mimicked. "It's true, isn't it, Baldwin? You are gay."

"I told you, my sexual preference is none of your concern, Miss D'Amour."

Amber laughed. "You know what, Baldwin? It's a good thing I'm feeling good right now, or I would be insulted." She stretched, again throwing her hip to one side and causing her pert, young breasts to push out against the T-shirt she was wearing. The prominent nipples showed that she wasn't wearing a bra. "Yes, sir, I'm feeling really good right now."

"It won't last," Baldwin said. "As soon as you come

down off that high, you'll be depressed again. Don't you know what that stuff does to you?"

"Yes, well, like you said, what I do with my life is of no concern of yours," Amber said petulantly. "I'm going to find a movie to watch."

"Enjoy," Baldwin said as Amber left the room.

On the surface, Baldwin Carter would seem to be an unlikely person to be affiliated with someone like Pablo Bustamante. But this wasn't a position thrust upon him by circumstances. Baldwin knew exactly what he was doing when he took the position of Bustamante's business manager.

Baldwin graduated from Mississippi State University, and got his MBA from Tulane. A short while ago he moved to Memphis, where he took a position with the accounting firm of Pierce, Trevathian, and Dunn, a Fortune 500 company.

One of PT&D's clients was Pablo Bustamante. It was precisely because of that client that Baldwin had begun working for Trevatian and Gunn. One he was in position, he took the first steps toward putting his plan into operation.

One day Trevathian was standing in front of his desk, holding a putter and leaning over a golf ball. Fifteen feet away from him was a glass turned upside down.

"Yes, Mr. Carter, what is it?" Trevathian asked as he surveyed the distance between himself and the glass.

"I've been going over the Bustamante account," Baldwin said.

Trevathian stroked the ball and it hit the glass. "Damn," he said. "Why can't I putt like that on the course? What about Bustamante's account?"

"We have been overbilling him," Baldwin said.

"Is that a fact?" Trevathian lined up for another putt.

"Yes, sir, and not by a small amount. Last year we overbilled him by some two and a half million dollars."

Again the ball hit the glass.

"Look at that!" Trevathian said triumphantly. He walked down to recover, not only the two balls that had hit the glass, but the six others that had missed and were nearby. Picking the eight balls up, he returned to his putting position. Not until then did he look up at Baldwin.

"Tell me, Mr. Carter. Do you know who Pablo Busta-mante is?" he asked.

"No, I don't," Baldwin replied. "Other than the fact that he is one of our largest clients."

"He is a drug dealer, Mr. Carter. He is a Hispanic-American who has contacts with the Medellin drug cartel in Colombia. He is one of the dregs of the earth, the scum at the bottom of humanity's pond."

"I wasn't aware of that."

"Perhaps we are overbilling him, but if so, where else can he go? A man like Bustamante has very few options."

"But do you think what we are doing is right?" Baldwin asked.

"Right?" Trevathian chuckled. "Look at it this way. The son of a bitch is getting away with his crime. We are just getting even for society. Do you have a problem with that, Mr. Carter?"

"No, sir," Baldwin said. "I don't have any problems with that."

"Good. Now, get back to work and let's hear nothing else about this overbilling."

One week later, Baldwin Carter, armed with printouts of all the facts and figures, took his vacation in Phoenix. There, he called the secret telephone number and got through directly to Bustamante.

"Yes?"

"Mr. Bustamante, you are being cheated out of two and a half million dollars per year," Baldwin said.

"Who is this?

"My name is Baldwin Carter. I work for Pierce, Trevathian, and Dunn. And I can save you two million dollars per year."

"I thought you said two and a half million," Bustamante said.

"Yes, sir, that is what I said. But if I'm going to go to work for you, my salary will be half a million a year."

There was a pause at the other end of the phone and for a moment, Baldwin thought he had overstepped himself. Then Bustamante laughed. "Where are you?" he asked.

"I'm at Sky Harbor Airport."

"I'll send a helicopter for you."

That was three years ago. Baldwin Carter had been a loyal employee ever since.

Amber D'Amour wasn't her real name. Her real name was Frances Butrum. Born a coal miner's daughter in rural West Virgina, she was both blessed and cursed with early maturation and beauty. By the age of twelve she was aware of the lecherous stares of men, by the age of thirteen she knew what the stares meant, and by the age of fourteen she had learned to capitalize on them.

Amber's father was killed in a mine explosion when she was sixteen, and her mother, who already lived her life as a shadow within shadows, withdrew further into herself. Amber left high school before she graduated, answering an ad for "attractive women who wish to enter the exciting and glamorous world of modeling."

Her modeling career did not pan out the way she thought it would. Instead of wearing beautiful clothes for photo spreads in elegant fashion magazines, she was forced to take "private modeling" projects.

Private modeling was the euphemism for posing naked for men, supposedly to do artistic photographs and drawings. More often than not, though, it was just to pander to their voyeuristic fetishes. Before she was eighteen, she was posing, nude, with legs spread, while men masturbated in front of her.

She graduated from posing to porn movies, and she met Pablo Bustamante at an exclusive private screening of one of her films. He was taken with her, and when he invited her to come with him, she did.

For the first few months it had been very good for her, and she actually began entertaining ideas of marrying him. She wasn't in love with him; love had nothing to do with it. She wanted to marry him because he was one of the wealthiest and most powerful men in America.

He didn't marry her, but he kept her in creature comforts and that was the next best thing. There was another bonus to living with one of the biggest drug dealers in America. Amber, who was a user, found an almost unending supply of what she needed.

Returning from Bustamante's meeting with Jahmshidi Mehdi, his private jet landed at Phoenix's Sky Harbor Airport. Deplaning from the jet, he boarded his private helicopter for the trip out to his house at Fountain Hills. There, he was met at the helipad by Baldwin.

"How did the meeting go?" Baldwin asked as the two started toward the house.

"It went well," Bustamante replied. "Jahmshidi has promised to provide our operation with an unlimited supply of raw material."

"Really?" Baldwin replied. "But at what price?"

"Ah, that's the good part, my friend. It won't cost us one penny."

Baldwin squinted his eyes in disbelief. "There has to be a catch to this," he said.

"No catch. It's called bartering. He does something for us, we will do something for him."

"What is he asking for?"

Bustamante shook his head. "You let me worry about that, my friend," he said. "I hired you for your financial advice. It is best for you to keep some separation between that and all other matters so that you can maintain a degree of . . . what is it the lawyers tell us? Credible deniability?"

"Yes, of course, Mr. Bustamante," Baldwin replied quickly. "I know you are looking out for my interests and I apologize for my curiosity."

"Where is Amber? I thought she would come out to meet me. She is here, isn't she?"

"Yes, sir. She's in the house."

"High?"

"I, uh, really couldn't say, sir."

"You're covering up for her."

"Not at all, sir. I just feel that it isn't my place to get involved."

"I keep telling her to get off that shit. I'm not high-minded about it. Hell, if everyone gave it up I'd be out of business. But I don't like the people who are around me to use it. That makes them less dependable."

"Yes, sir," Baldwin said without elaboration.

By now they were in the house, in the huge den that had a picture window as large as the side wall of an ordinary house. The window opened up onto a beautiful mountain view and even now, as a golden sun was setting, they were treated to a glorious vista of purple mountains and orange, red, and lavender clouds.

Amber was waiting in the great room for them, and as soon as Bustamante came in, she began preparing a drink for him. He settled on one of the sofas. Baldwin had not been invited to sit, so he remained standing. Bustamante looked up at him.

"So, tell me, Baldwin, how goes our operation?"

"We are doing very well," Baldwin replied. "Our primary business is up fourteen percent over this time last year."

Bustamante interrupted with a laugh. "So much for the 'war on drugs,'" he said. "Of course, it doesn't hurt our cause to have high-profile people arguing for legalization of drugs."

"But legalizing drugs would be bad for our business," Baldwin said.

"Oh, you don't have to worry about that. Drugs will never be legalized. But having well-known Hollywood personalities favoring legalization takes away some of the stigma of using drugs. That will break down the inhibitions of some of the more cautious, creating a larger customer base."

"True," Baldwin replied.

"And what about the whores on wheels?"

"By whores on wheels, I take it you are referring to the procurement operation?" Baldwin asked.

Bustamante chuckled. "Procurement, yes, if that's what you want to call it."

"It is also showing a healthy profit," Baldwin reported.

"I thought it would be. We were paid handsomely for the girls I just delivered to Sitarkistan. And the beauty of that is, we didn't sell the girls to them, we merely leased them. That was one of your better ideas."

"Yes," Baldwin agreed. "By leasing them, we are no different from a temporary employment agency. That allows us to maintain control over them. And though it is a technicality, it also allows us to avoid an international charge of white slavery."

"Yes, well, I have no sympathy for the women. Most of them are better off than they were before we recruited them. I mean, think about it. They answered our ads in the first place because they were poor, starving, and overworked in some Third World country."

"Yes, sir. They answer the ads, thinking they are going to marry a rich American," Baldwin said. "Instead, they wind up in some sex harem in the Middle East."

"Why, Baldwin, is that a criticism?" Bustamante asked.

"I'm not that proud of our involvement in it," Baldwin said.

"If you liked women, you would be more tolerant of our involvement."

"Perhaps so," Baldwin said.

"Anyway, I look at it as a service. Not only for the men who are able to enjoy the company of beautiful women, but for the women themselves."

"A service to the women?"

"Look at it this way, Baldwin. Once there, the women are pampered and fed and clothed. If you went to one hundred of them, ninety-nine would tell you that they prefer being where they are now to where they were."

"Still, there is that one," Baldwin said.

"Whoa now," Bustamante said. "You aren't going soft on me, are you, Baldwin?"

"No!" Baldwin replied. "Not even a little bit," he added quickly, frightened that he might have said too much. He cleared his throat. "Anyway, to continue with my report, the, uh, procurement operation is also up over last year," he concluded.

"Tell me this, my friend. Are we beating the Dow?" Bustamante asked.

Baldwin laughed out loud. "Yes. And the S&P and NASDAQ," he said.

Giving the drink to Bustamante, Amber turned toward Baldwin. "Baldwin," she said. "Get lost. I want to welcome Pablo back home."

"What?" Baldwin replied.

Amber began unbuttoning her blouse.

"I said get lost," she said. Unabashedly, she removed the blouse, baring her breasts.

"Oh, uh, yes," Baldwin said, now growing embarrassed. "Yes, of course."

Baldwin hurried out of the room, even as he saw Amber straddling Bustamante.

"Pablo, what did you mean when you said you wanted Baldwin to be able to have credible deniability?"

Having satisfied Bustamante's immediate needs, she was now sitting, naked, on the opposite end of the couch from him. She took a sip of her own drink.

"It just means that if I do something that I keep him in the dark about, he can't be an accomplice for it if the cops ever arrest him."

"So, what are you not telling him about this trip?" Amber asked.

Pablo chuckled. "You mean you don't want the protection of credible deniability?"

"Baby, whatever happens to you, happens to me," Amber purred.

"All right. We'll just see about that. I've made a deal with Jahmshidi Mehdi to conduct a few paramilitary operations for him."

"Paramilitary operations?"

"Some might call them terrorist operations."

"You mean like the Palestinians and all that?"

"Not exactly," Bustamante replied. He laughed. "I can't promise anyone who does this for me immediate passage into heaven. But that's all right because none of them would know what to do with seventy-two virgins anyway. Hell, most of them wouldn't know what to do with one virgin. So, I won't be asking them to martyr themselves."

"Then what will you be asking them to do?"

"Make a show," he said. "Plant a few bombs, that sort of thing. Just enough to let Jahmshidi know that I'm holding up my end of the bargain."

"Do you think you can get people to do something like that?"

"You can get people to do a lot of things if you pay enough," Bustamante said.

"How much are you going to pay?" Amber asked.

"It depends on what they are willing to do," Bustamante replied. "Why do you ask? Are you interested in doing something?"

"I might be interested," Amber admitted. "It sounds" — she hugged herself, then shivered—"wickedly exciting."

Seven

To his neighbors, Rubin Dockins was a friendly man who always returned a wave, who often came to the neighborhood sports bar to drink beer, eat popcorn, and get into good-natured arguments over the ball games. He was a farm-equipment salesman who worked on commission out of his own home, so he could set his own hours, but his job required frequent travel. He was unmarried, and more than one single or divorced woman in the neighborhood had dropped hints that she would be available if he wanted to call.

What the neighbors did not know was that Rubin's farm-equipment job was a front for what he really did. Rubin was an enforcer . . . a "hitter," who did freelance work for anyone who was willing to pay.

He charged a lot for his services, but he was very good at it. A former sniper for the U.S. Army, Rubin had been dishonorably discharged from the service nine years ago for committing statutory rape against the daughter of a colonel.

The irony was, she had come on to him. Maybe she was only fifteen at the time, but if so, Rubin had news for the colonel. His daughter was no innocent, young virgin.

She had been with a man long before Rubin Dockins ever met her.

Rubin lived in an upper-middle-class neighborhood in a ranch-style house with a deep front yard. As he pulled into his driveway, he saw his neighbor, Walt, washing his car.

"Hey, Walt, what are you doing washing your car? Isn't Kansas State playing?" he called.

"They don't play until four," Walt said. "But they'll be playing Nebraska, so I don't know if I have the stomach to watch it."

Rubin chuckled. "Well, if you get your nerve up, give me a call. We'll go down to the sports bar and watch with some of the others."

"Sounds good. How was your trip to Denver?" Walt asked.

"Good. Very good," Rubin said. "I made the sale."

"Well, then, you'll be buying the beer tonight, right?"

"I'll do better than that. I'll even buy your dinner. And I'll sympathize with you for your loss to Nebraska."

"Oh, you are a cruel man for even bringing that up," his neighbor said, and Rubin laughed as he headed for his house.

Rubin thought about the job he had just completed. It was a county commissioner in California, an influential man who was on the take from the mob, but had gotten greedy. Rubin was paid ten thousand dollars to take care of the situation.

Covering his tracks, Rubin bought a round-trip ticket from Kansas City to Denver. While in Denver, he rented a car and drove down Highway 83 to the little town of Parker, where he sold a combine to a farmer. Then he flew to Bakersfield, California, where he transferred to a pickup truck that was left in a predetermined location. Behind the seat of the pickup truck was an

Enfield .303 rifle, with a scope, a picture of his target, and his address, which was a house about ten miles out of town.

Rubin drove to the address to scout the job and saw, with some satisfaction, that there were no other houses anywhere close. He stopped the truck about five hundred yards away from the house, raised the hood, and began looking at the engine. When the commissioner walked down to check his mailbox, he didn't even glance toward the pickup. Rubin stepped around behind the truck, aimed, and fired.

The commissioner went down with a bullet in his heart, dead before he even hit the ground.

"One shot, one kill," Rubin said aloud.

Almost leisurely, Rubin put the hood down and returned to Bakersfield, where he ran the pickup through a car wash, before leaving it where he'd gotten it. One hour later he was on a plane back to Denver, where he used the other half of his ticket for the flight back to Kansas City.

Rubin got his "special" assignments through the Internet, where he maintained a website called www.rubin ops.com. The website was a totally black page with only three words, in red, plus a link that would enable someone to send him e-mail.

The three words were:

Situations satisfactorily arranged.

Most of the e-mail he received consisted of missives questioning him about his site, asking for an explanation. He discarded that mail. But this morning he opened an e-mail that had nothing but a telephone number.

He dialed the number.

"Hello?" The voice at the other end was hesitant and questioning.

"I got your e-mail," Rubin said.

"I almost didn't answer. There's nothing on my caller ID."

"I like to keep it that way."

"I need a job done."

"What kind of job?"

"First, let me tell you how much I'll pay."

"All right."

"One hundred thousand dollars."

Rubin whistled softly. "Must be one hell of a job."

"Can you access your e-mail while you are on the phone?"

"Yes."

"All right. I'm sending you the particulars. Don't hang up."

Rubin glanced down at his laptop and saw the little flag come up. He opened the e-mail.

"Upon your acceptance of the job, an immediate electronic transfer of one hundred thousand will be made to your account."

"Did you get that?" his contact asked over the phone.

"Yeah. You still haven't said what the job is. Who—"

"Ask all questions by e-mail."

Rubin typed in his message.

"Who do you want me to kill?"

The response came back.

"I don't care."

"What do you mean, you don't care?" Rubin replied over the phone. "That doesn't make sense."

"It makes sense to me. All I care about is that you kill ten people. Any ten, anywhere."

Rubin stared at the e-mail. This whole thing was getting more confusing by the minute.

"Let me get this straight. You are going to pay me one hun-

dred thousand dollars to kill ten people, but you don't care who the ten are, or where I kill them?"

"That's right," his contact answered over the phone.

"Why?"

"You don't need to know that," his contact replied. Again, he typed in a message.

"Do you remember the sniping incident around Washington, D.C., a few years ago?"

Rubin typed back.

"Yes. Some dumb-assed kid. An amateur. He shot thirteen times, only killed ten."

His contact replied. *"Ten kills out of thirteen shots sounds pretty good to me."*

Rubin typed, *"One shot, one kill."*

"What is that? Some sort of motto?"

"It's the Army sniper's creed."

"Well, whether he killed nine or thirteen, the point is, for several days the entire Washington area was paralyzed with fear. People were afraid to put gas in their cars, or go shopping, or to a restaurant. Do you think you could do that?"

"Yes, I can do that. Where do you want me to go?"

"I told you, you can pick your own city. What I want is for you to bring it to a halt the way those two did to Washington, D.C."

"Any city I want?"

"Yes."

"Good. Then I pick Mobile."

"Mobile? Mobile, Alabama?"

"Yes."

"Well, I did say you could pick any city you want but why Mobile?"

"I have my reasons."

"All right, Mobile it is. So long as you cause a panic."

"Oh, I expect I'll frighten a few people all right. Who are you?"

"It isn't important that you know who I am. Once you see the first transfer of money, you will know that I am serious."

"That's good enough for me," Rubin said.

Rubin hung up the phone, shut down his computer, and began packing for Mobile. It had been a long time coming, but he was about to settle an old score.

Retired Army Colonel Emile D. Virden lived in Mobile. Virden was the father of the girl Dockins had "raped." Virden and his wife had bought a large turn-of-the-century mansion in the historic Oakleigh District, and fixed it up as a bed-and-breakfast. It couldn't be good for his business if people started getting shot nearby.

It had been nine years since the incident, but Dockins chuckled, as he thought of an old adage. *Vengeance is a dish best served cold.*

Pablo Bustamante hung up the phone. Rubin Dockins was a start, but only a start. The most he would be able to accomplish with the sniping was cause a panic. Creating a panic would be effective, but he needed to augment that with some other demonstrations, perhaps something a little more dramatic. And to do that, he needed someone with the commitment of a fanatical Muslim.

Chicago, Illinois

Cesar Adib Jubair was an immigrant from Mindanao, the Philippines. Because he was Filipino, and looked Filipino rather than Arab, most thought he was Roman Catholic, until they heard his name. Jubair lived in the U.S., and had for several years. He had come to the U.S. for the economic opportunity, but so far his economic opportunity consisted of working in car washes, fast-food restaurants, and as a bag boy in grocery stores. He hated Americans. He hated the way they drove their fine cars and wore expensive clothing and acted as if you weren't even there. He hated the way they doted on their children and how they obsessed on their sports teams, and how the women flaunted their sexuality without the slightest shame. And now, with Christmas season approaching, and their orgy of "buying for Jesus," he hated them even more.

He had quietly applauded when the hijackers flew into the World Trade Center. He admired them, and sympathized with their action, but wasn't so committed that he would martyr himself.

He heard about the unique opportunity offered by Pablo Bustamante from a friend at the mosque.

"I know a way you can make a lot of money," Suliman Jabar told him. Before Lorenzo Montjoy converted to Islam and changed his name to Suliman Abdul, he had been a one-time player and a drug dealer. Suliman had cleaned himself up when he became a Muslim, but he still maintained contact with the street, and with many of his old friends who were still in the drug culture. It was from them that he'd heard of Pablo Bustamante's offer.

Suliman had no desire to kill anyone. It wasn't that he wouldn't kill. He had killed in the past, but he had never killed without reason. One of his victims had tried to cheat him out of his money; another had been trying to make a power grab. But the information that he had about Bustamante was that he wanted some people who could plant a few bombs in places that would cause a lot of casualties.

Suliman didn't know why Bustamante wanted such a thing done, but concluded that it must have something to do with him expanding his business. That didn't matter to Suliman. He was no longer interested in drugs, or territory. But he had had several discussions with Jubair, and he knew that Jubair burned to strike out against the unbelievers.

"How do I contact this person?" Jubair asked.

"You don't contact somebody like Pablo Bustamante," Suliman told him. "The only thing you can do is sit back and hope that he contacts you."

"How can that be? He doesn't know me."

"He will contact you," Suliman said cryptically.

To Jubair's complete surprise, the initial contact happened that very night.

"You are Jubair?" a voice at the other end of the phone asked.

"Yes."

"Do you know what I want from you?"

"I think I know. You want me to—"

"Don't say it over the telephone," the voice said. "Do you know the Land of Lincoln Storage Company on Eighteenth?"

"No."

"Well, do you think you can find it?" the voice asked in exasperation.

"Yes."

"Good. A key is being mailed to you. That key is to Unit 271 of the Lincoln Storage Company. Go to the unit, and follow the instructions you'll find inside."

"What about the money?"

"Along with the instructions, there will be a telephone number for you to call to authorize an electronic transfer of funds to your account. Do you understand all your instructions so far?"

"Yes."

"If you do not carry out your instructions within three

days of transferring the money, we will have you killed. Do you understand that?"

"Yes."

"Do you accept these terms?"

"Yes. I accept them," Jubair answered.

Clopton, Alabama

Dexter Pogue was thirty-five years old. Although he called himself a construction worker, he had been fired by three contractors and worked only when one of them needed an extra man for a day or two. He had also tried to sell used cars, but because his salary depended upon commissions earned, was let go after three months with no sale.

He managed to collect a little disability from a shoulder injury he had sustained on one of his construction jobs, and he augmented that by working at various fast-food places, rarely staying more than two weeks.

Pogue drove a 1982 pickup truck, which was a visual testimony to his philosophy. The window of his pickup was filled with NASCAR stickers, including the number 3 for Dale Ernhardt. His bumper stickers reflected his politics.

"I'll give up my gun when they pry it from my cold, dead hands."

"This truck does not brake for liberals."

"Clean up the environment, nuke Washington."

"Bill Clinton saved our country by sticking his finger in a dyke."

A confederate flag flew from the top of an oversized CB antennae, and he swore he would shoot anyone who tried to take it down. To help him carry out that task, he had a gun rack in his back window where he kept a .30-30 lever-action Winchester, and a 12-gauge Boss shotgun. He also carried one pistol stuck down in his belt and another in his right boot, though he had no permit to do so.

Pogue hung out at a bar called Hog's Breath, where he kept up a running diatribe against the government in general . . . and Senator Harriet Clayton in particular. Even among the other customers of Hog's Breath, nearly all of whom were staunchly conservative and chagrined at the idea that Harriet Clayton might actually be elected President someday, his vitriol was beginning to wear thin.

Then one day, as Pogue sat in a booth at the back of the Hog's Breath with a man named Harley Sumlin, Sumlin challenged him.

"You serious about wantin' to do somthin' about that Clayton bitch? Or are you just a-runnin' off at the mouth?" Sumlin asked. Sumlin was Pogue's local connection for marijuana.

"What do you mean by do somethin'?" Pogue asked.

"I mean do somthin'," Sumlin replied. "You can make a lot of money if you are serious. I mean a lot of money. But it's goin' to take a pair of balls."

"Yeah? Well, I got balls like an elephant," Pogue said.

"Oh, you do."

"You damn straight I do. Now just what the fuck are you talking' about?"

"Hang loose, Pogue. Just hang loose. Somebody will contact you."

"Who?" Pogue asked. He drained the last of his beer, then pointed at Sumlin. "It better not be no Yankee sumbitch," he said. "I ain't dealin' with no Yankee sumbitch."

"Yankee money spends as good as Southern money, don't it?" Sumlin asked.

Pogue thought for a moment, then nodded. "Yeah, I reckon it does," he said. "What's all this about anyhow?"

"Like I told you. Just hang loose for a while," Sumlin said. "Somebody will get ahold of you."

"You say there's money to be made?"

"Lots of money," Sumlin said.

"Enough for me to buy a new truck?"

"Enough for you to buy twenty new trucks."

Eight

Mobile, Alabama

The house was on Dauphin Street, an old house bristling with cupolas, dormers, and gingerbread woodwork that had stood empty for nearly ten years. Now the house was boarded up while the estate decided whether to spend money to renovate it for rent or sale, or tear it down and sell the lot the sprawling house occupied.

The moment Dockins saw the house, he realized it would be perfect for him. With the dormers and a full attic, it was three stories high. Looking at the dormers, he saw that if he used one of them as his firing platform, he would have the exact elevation he needed to select and fire upon targets at the corner intersection. And the good thing was, it was within two blocks of Virden's bed-and-breakfast.

Having found his shooting perch, the next thing he needed to do was explore the neighborhood, to find a place to park his car. He also needed an unobstructed egress from the house and a means of moving, unobserved, from the house to his car.

He found what he was looking for two blocks away from the house, on the street behind the house. The alley was bordered on either side by high fences, and on one side there was a long thick growth of shrubbery with enough room between the shrubbery and the fence to allow him passage.

With the preliminary business taken care of, Dockins found a motel. He would stay there until just before dawn the next morning. He would use the cover of predawn darkness to get into the house, though he would make his shot in the daytime, probably during the morning rush hour.

One shot, one kill.

Before he went to his room, Dockins stopped at an outdoor pay phone and called a number he had already looked up.

"Virden's Bed and Breakfast," a man's voice answered. It was Colonel Virden's voice.

Dockins said nothing.

"Hello?" Virden's voice said.

Dockins remained quiet.

"This is Virden's Bed and Breakfast," Virden said again.

"One shot, one kill," Dockins said, whispering in a hoarse voice.

"What? Who is this?" Virden asked.

Dockins hung up the phone without saying a word. For a long moment, he considered making Virden his target, but decided against it because it would have been possible to trace the killing back to him. After all, Virden was a former commandant of the sniper school. Had he been killed by a sniper, good detective work would reason that an ex-sniper was acting out an old grudge. And it wouldn't take much to learn that Dockins had been dishonorably discharged for the incident with Virden's daughter.

No, he wouldn't shoot Virden. But he was certain that the thought of a disgruntled sniper running loose in his city would cause Virden some uncomfortable moments.

* * *

Virden's Bed and Breakfast

Emile Virden hung up the phone and stared at it for a long moment.

"Who was it, dear?" his wife asked. "Who called?"

"I don't know," Virden said. He checked the caller ID, then dialed the number back. There was no answer.

"Emile, is everything all right?" Millie asked, stepping out into the foyer.

"Yes, I think so," Emile replied. Going over to the computer, he called up a reverse-number program and saw that he had been called from a public pay phone.

The caller had said, "One shot, one kill."

Colonel Emile Virden was former commandant of the U.S. Army Special Operations Force Target Interdiction Course at Ft. Bragg, North Carolina. Target interdiction was military terminology for sniper operations, and the unofficial motto of the snipers was, "One shot, one kill."

The call could not have been mere coincidence. It had to be related to Virden's former position. On the other hand, it didn't have the tone of someone who wanted to hash over old times. On the contrary, there was something rather ominous about the call.

"Emile, are you sure you are all right?" Millie asked.

"Yes, I'm fine," Emile said, closing down the website. He smiled. "What's for supper?"

It was a little after eight o'clock the next morning when Dockins's first target of opportunity presented itself. Actually, it was targets of opportunity, for two motorcycle policemen, riding side by side, had stopped for the traffic light. There were other cars waiting for the light, as well as cars passing through the intersection.

The setup was perfect. He had an excellent field of fire, traffic noise would mask the sound so that people would not be able to tell where his shot came from, and in the confusion he would be able to get away. Releasing the safety, Dockins took aim at the policeman farthest away. When he had a perfect sight picture, he squeezed the trigger.

Sue Patterson was sitting across the intersection from the two policemen, waiting for the light to change. Seeing the policemen reminded her that she had not gotten around to renewing her driver's license, and she had the irrational thought that they might suddenly start checking for licenses.

Then, as she was watching them, a strange thing happened . . . something that was so foreign to her experience or expectation that, for a moment, she had no idea what she was seeing. A spray of red suddenly erupted from the side of the head of one of the policemen. The policeman fell from his motorcycle, and the bike fell over with him.

Still not sure of what she had just seen, Sue stared in shock and confusion as the second policeman set the stand on his own bike and got off to see about his partner. He took one step toward the fallen officer when his own head exploded in a cloud of red spray.

Now panic took over and Sue pressed down on the accelerator to get away, but the light had not yet changed and, in order to miss her, an oncoming truck swerved and hit a fire hydrant. A plume of water spewed high into the air, and the truck's horn began to honk unceasingly.

In the resultant confusion, Dockins found it very easy to get away.

That evening, Dockins called Virden again.

"Virden's Bed and Breakfast," Colonel Virden said.

"You taught me well, Colonel. Did you see my handiwork on the news today?" Again, Dockins spoke in a low, hoarse voice.

"What? Who is this?"

"One shot, one kill," Dockins said. "Except today, it was two shots, two kills."

"My God! Are you telling me you are the one who killed those two policemen?"

Dockins hung up without saying another word.

Code Name Team Headquarters

John Barrone, Mike Rojas, Don Yee, and Wagner were back in the computer room, where Don, who was the team's computer guru, was showing off a new piece of equipment. Jennifer Barnes, Linda Marsh, and Chris Farmer were in the living room, watching the evening news. On-screen, Harriet Clayton was smiling and waving at all the beautiful people.

"Don't wave at me, bitch," Jennifer said to the screen. "You make my ass knit barbed wire."

Linda laughed. "Come on, Jennifer, tell us what you really think of her."

"Surely that woman won't be elected President, will she? Surely the country is smarter than that."

"She's got quite a following," Chris replied. "Most people think her husband got as high as he did because of Harriet."

"Yuk," Jennifer said.

"In Mobile, Alabama, today, two police officers were killed in a sniper-type shooting incident," the TV announcer said. "There is no known motive for the shooting, though the killer is said to have left a note with the cryptic message 'One shot, one kill.'"

"What did he just say?" Chris asked, leaning forward in his seat.

"He said, 'One shot, one kill,'" Jennifer said. "Why? Does that mean something to you?"

"Yeah," Chris said. He leaned back in his seat. "Yeah, it does."

"Well?" Jennifer asked.

"Well what?" Chris replied.

Jennifer chuckled. "What does it mean?"

"Oh. It's the motto of the U.S. Army sniper," Chris said without elaboration.

Thirty-six hours after the first shooting, Dockins struck again, this time killing a husband and wife as they were waiting to cross the street. Again, that night, he called Virden.

"One shot, one kill," he said.

"You murdering bastard. If you went through the target-interdiction course, you are a disgrace to the brave men who have served in that duty," Virden said angrily.

Dockins hung up, then left the public phone and drove to another motel.

Forty-eight hours later, he killed a businessman as the businessman was leaving a restaurant.

"I am the product of your school, Colonel," Dockins said in the telephone call he made that evening. "Are you proud of your handiwork?"

Colonel Virden's daughter was now happily married and living in Seattle, the mother of twins. The colonel and his family had spent nine years trying to put the statutory rape incident out of their minds; thus Virden could be excused for not immediately figuring out who the sniper was. But a process of elimination led him to the conclusion that it had to be Rubin Dockins. So this time, when Dockins called, Virden was ready for him.

"Dockins, you were a worthless piece of shit when you were in my command, and you are even more worthless now," he said.

There was a gasp, then a moment of silence from the other end of the line.

"Dockins?" Colonel Virden said.

"Well, well, well. Congratulations, Colonel," Dockins said. "I didn't think you would be able figure it out. You outsmarted me."

"A person doesn't have to be too intelligent to outsmart you."

"Yeah? Well, what are you going to do about it, Colonel? Tell the FBI?" He laughed. "Do you think they can stop me?"

FBI Field Office, Mobile

Agent Andy Morris dropped a file folder on the station chief's desk.

"It's just like you thought," Morris said. "This guy Virden has a long-standing grudge against Rubin Dockins."

"What do we have on Dockins?"

Morris shook his head. "Mr. Dockins lives in Kansas City, Missouri. He is a model citizen, a farm-equipment salesmen, and has been as clean as a whistle ever since he was discharged. Even his military record was exemplary until the incident with the colonel's daughter."

"Contact our people in Kansas City, have one of them run him down and talk to him."

"Well, I did that, but he wasn't there. His neighbors say that he is often on the road selling equipment and is sometimes gone for several days at a time. There's nothing unusual in this."

"He's not on any sex-offender watch, is he?"

"No, it wasn't forcible rape, it was statutory. And by all accounts, the girl was willing. According to the Universal Code of Military Justice, the age of consent is only sixteen, and this happened on a military base. If it had happened four weeks later, the girl would have been legal and there is nothing they could've done to Dockins."

The station chief studied the file for a moment longer. "I'd feel a little better if we had been able to speak to him."

"Oh, we have spoken to him," Morris said.

The station chief looked up. "I thought you said he was gone."

"He is, but they reached him on his cell phone. He's somewhere in Nebraska."

The station chief stroked his chin in contemplation. "All right, I tell you what. Get Virden's permission to put a tap on his phone. If he really is getting calls, let's listen in to a few of them."

"All right," Morris said.

Twenty-four hours later, a schoolteacher was taking her first-grade class on a field trip to visit a public library. The children were hanging on to a long rope as a means of keeping them all together, and the teacher was in front, leading them.

"Now, wait for the light," the teacher explained. "When it is green, we will cross the street. Move quickly, but don't run."

"The light *is* green," one little boy said.

"No, John, you are looking at the light from the other direction. This is the light for us, and it is red, do you see?" She pointed.

"Yes, ma'am. I see."

"Now, don't go until—" Suddenly there was a snapping sound, and the teacher gasped once, got a surprised expression on her face, then looked down at her chest. He blouse was already red with blood. She put her hand over her wound, trying to stanch the flow of blood, but it spilled rapidly through her fingers. She fell facedown while the children, still hanging on to the rope, looked on in fear and confusion.

Colonel Virden was sitting at the computer when the phone rang, and once more he typed the number from the caller ID to see where the call was coming from. Like the other calls, this one had been placed from a public phone, though not from the same phone as the others. Dockins was obviously moving around the city.

"Damn!" Virden said in disgust, even as he was picking up the telephone.

Recognizing the frustration in Virden's voice, Dockins chuckled. "What were you trying to do, Colonel? Trying to trace this call?"

"Something like that," Virden replied.

"With caller ID, you think I'd be foolish enough to call you from where I'm staying? I'm at a public phone on the corner of Third and Semmes. But of course, I'm sure you already know that."

"What do you want, Dockins?" Virden asked. "Why are you calling me?"

"I want to know how you feel, knowing that you are responsible for all these deaths?" Dockins asked.

"What do you mean I am responsible? How the hell am I responsible?"

"Oh, you are responsible all right," Dockins replied.

"First you taught me how to shoot. Then you took me to the Gulf and taught me how to kill."

"Nobody taught you how to kill, you sick son of a bitch," Colonel Virden said. "You were a loose cannon who got off on killing. You started killing indiscriminately, not priority targets, but ordinary soldiers at their morning toilet."

"Ordinary enemy soldiers," Dockins said.

"Enemy or not, they were human beings. And you weren't killing them as an act of war, you were just killing them. That's why I pulled you off-line."

"And cost me my promotion," Dockins said.

"I should've thrown your ass in the stockade. Maybe if I had, you wouldn't have gotten into trouble later."

"Oh, are you talking about what happened with your slut of a daughter? I tried to tell you then that she's the one who came on to me. Everybody on the post was fucking her, but I'm the one you came after."

"Is that what this is all about? Are you carrying out a nine-year-old grudge against me by killing innocent people?"

"No, sir, Colonel, this is much more than a grudge. You see, I've signed on to a holy war. I'm getting paid for this. What you think about that, Colonel Virden? Killing for fun and profit. I mean, when you think about it, that's a hell of a thing, isn't it?" Dockins laughed again. "And the best thing is . . . there is nothing you, or anyone else, can do about it."

"That's where you are wrong, buddy boy. I am going to do something about it. I'm going to nail your ass to my garage door."

"Oh? And how are you going to do that?"

"One shot, one kill," Virden said.

"Wait a minute! Are you telling me that you are coming after me? You? Well, bring it on, Colonel! I welcome the challenge."

"I will see you dead, Dockins. You will not get out of this town alive."

"Like I said, bring it on."

Colonel Virden slammed the phone down in anger. Within seconds it rang again. This time the caller ID read, "ID withheld." He knew it was the FBI.

"Did you hear it?" he asked.

"Yes," Morris said.

"Do you believe me now?"

"Yes," Morris said again. "We've already got someone on the way to the phone he used."

"He'll be gone."

"Colonel, what did you mean when you said he would not leave this town alive?"

"I didn't mean anything by it," Colonel Virden said. "It's just a form of psychological warfare."

"I would advise you not to try anything on your own."

"I'm sixty-six years old, Agent Morris. That's a little old for war games. No, sir, catching this son of a bitch is your job."

"I'm glad you see it that way," Agent Morris said.

"So, other than putting a tap on my phone, what else are you doing?"

"We're doing everything we can," Morris replied. "Don't worry, these guys always slip up. Look what happened to the D.C. snipers."

"They were amateurs," Virden said. "This man is a professional. I know, because I trained him."

"You say that almost with pride, Colonel," Morris said.

After he hung up the phone, Dockins went into the quick-service store and bought a six-pack of beer, then drove around looking for another motel. He had changed motels every night so he wouldn't be staying in one place long enough for someone to remember him.

He took the beer up to his room, opened a can, then turned on the TV to watch the news.

The graphic of crosshairs came onto the screen, and the screen took on a red tint as they began playing the music that was the introductory theme. Chuckling, Dockins hummed the theme along with the TV.

"The Mobile sniper struck again," a somber-voiced newscaster began.

Dockins watched the story, then began surfing through the channels until he found it somewhere else. The Mobile chief of police was being interviewed.

"Do we want this guy? You damn right we want him. I remind you that his first two victims were Mobile policemen."

"What about the FBI?"

"My department is cooperating fully with the FBI," the chief said.

"Do you have any leads?" the interviewer asked.

"Nothing new, but we'll get him. You may recall, the D.C. snipers thought they were getting away with it, but they were caught. So will this person, or persons, be caught."

"Ha," Dockins said to the TV screen. "You've got about as much chance as Colonel Virden. I wish that old fool *would* come after me."

Nine

Dockins had totally misunderstood the nature of Colonel Virden's challenge. Colonel Virden's military background was as a leader. He didn't do things himself. He got someone else to do things for him. And he knew just the person for this job.

Rubin Dockins had made the boast that he was the best of all the men who went through the Target Interdiction Course. Virden had let him mouth off, but Virden knew that wasn't right. Of all the soldiers Virden had trained and commanded, the best, and the one of whom he was most proud, was Chris Farmer.

During the first Gulf War, Colonel Virden was ordered to assemble a cadre of his best snipers and command them for a special operation. Sergeant Chris Farmer was the most successful of those snipers, killing seventeen Iraqi soldiers, including nine high-ranking officers of Saddam's Special Guard. Not one of Chris's shots had been made from inside one thousand yards.

Virden had kept up with Chris all these years. He knew that Chris was with some sort of agency that undertook difficult assignments. He had heard of the agency, the Code Name Team, most recently when it had been mentioned by Senator Harriet Clayton. But he honestly didn't know if the Code Name Team was government-sponsored, or a private agency.

At this point, he didn't care. He wanted Dockins handled, so he called a friend who was a member of the Army Security Agency, the Army's equivalent of the CIA.

"Burton," the voice said.

Emile knew that Burton was a lieutenant colonel, but like soldiers in the CID, soldiers in the ASA never revealed their rank. Burton had once been a young second lieutenant in one of Emile's earlier commands. Emile had taken a liking to the young lieutenant, and helped him through some difficult times.

"Sandy, this is Emile Virden."

"Colonel Virden, it's great to hear your voice," Burton said with genuine enthusiasm.

The two men exchanged pleasantries for a few moments. Then Emile got around to the reason for his call.

Burton chuckled. "I didn't think you were just trying to catch up on old times," he said. "What can I do for you?"

"I'm trying to get hold of someone who used to serve under me. He was a sergeant then, but he's a civilian now."

"Is there some reason why you think I might be able to help you?" Burton asked.

"Yes," Emile replied. "I believe he is affiliated with something called the Code Name Team. Have you ever heard of it?"

Now the joviality left Burton's voice, and when he answered this time, it was flat and professional. "Yes," he said. "I've heard of it."

"Is that an official government agency?" Emile asked.

"I'm not sure. I know it has nothing to do with the Army. Who are you looking for?"

"His name is Farmer. Sergeant Chris Farmer."

"I'll see what I can do," Burton replied. "Stand by your phone."

* * *

Code Name Team Headquarters:

It was less than thirty minutes later when Chris Farmer's cell phone rang. Chris checked the caller ID. It was a number her knew from memory.

"Well, this is a voice from the past," Chris answered. "Hello, Colonel Virden."

"It has been a long time," Emile Virden said. "Hello, Sergeant Farmer."

Chris chuckled. "So long that nobody ever calls me Sergeant anymore. What are you up to these days? Retired by now, I'm sure."

"Yes."

Chris chuckled. "That's good. I thought maybe you were wanting to reactivate me for a mission."

"Funny you would say that," Colonel Virden said.

"Oh? What is it? What's up?"

"I'm in Mobile, Alabama, Chris. Since I'm calling you on your cell phone, I don't know where you are. But you'd almost have to be on the backside of the moon not to be aware of what's been going on here."

"You're talking about the 'one shot, one kill' sniper?"

"Yes."

"He's one of us, isn't he?"

"Yes," Emile said again.

"Who is it?"

"It's Rubin Dockins. I'm sure you remember him."

There was a moment of silence on Chris's end of the line. Then he sighed. "Yes, sir, I remember him. He was on my fire team in Iraq."

"I know."

"He was a pretty good soldier as I recall. The only thing, he seemed to enjoy his work just a little too much. I lost track of him after I left the Army. Is he still in?"

"No, he, uh, got into some trouble and picked up a dishonorable discharge," Virden said rather self-consciously.

"How do you know he is the sniper?"

"He told me."

"Dockins told you?"

"Yes. He's been calling me, Chris. After every shoot."

"Why would he do that?"

"He said he was doing it because he wanted me to feel guilty about the victims he was shooting."

"Let me get this straight. He's on this killing spree just to make you feel guilty?"

"Partly. He also said that he is being paid to kill. 'Killing for fun and profit,' is how he put it. That part doesn't make any sense to me. I don't know who would pay him to kill randomly, or why they would do it, but that is what he said."

"Have you been to the police with this information?"

"I went to the FBI with it. They've put a tap on my phone, but they don't seem close to getting him."

"What do you want with me, Colonel?" Chris asked.

Virden paused for a moment, then took a deep breath. "I want him interdicted."

Chris was silent for a moment.

"Look, I know you two served together," Colonel Virden continued. "And I can understand how you might be a little squeamish about interdicting one of your own. But I get the feeling that he is going to continue killing until he is stopped."

"Yeah, I did serve with him," Chris said. "If, as he said, he is getting paid to do this, it has become a depersonalized mission for him. And I've never known anyone who was more mission-oriented than Rubin Dockins. So you are right. He will continue killing until his mission is done, or until someone stops him."

"Then you agree that he has to be stopped?"

"Yes, sir. I agree."

"Will you take the assignment?"

"I feel as responsible for him as you do, Colonel. So my answer is yes. I'll take the assignment."

"Thanks," Colonel Virden said.

"Wait a minute, Chris," John said. "You know our policy. Nobody freelances, nobody goes out on their own. Anything that any of us take on, all of us take on."

"Yeah, well, the thing is, Colonel Virden asked me personally," Chris said. "And I feel obligated to him."

"Why do you feel obligated?" Jennifer asked. "Did he save your life or something?"

"No," Chris replied. He looked over toward Wagner. "Wagner has never saved my life either, but if it had been him instead of Colonel Virden, I would do it for him. It's a matter of loyalty."

"It's more than that," Mike said. "It's a matter of honor. I say this becomes a Code Team Operation."

"Are you asking us to take it on?" John asked.

"No," Chris replied. "Well, yes, but I want to be the point man."

"Is there a possibility you are too close to this?" Wagner asked. "I mean, by your own admission, you served with this man."

"Yes," Chris said.

"How close were you?" Lana asked.

"We shared MREs, drank from the same canteen, covered each other's back," Chris said. He was quiet for a moment. Then he added, "And he saved my life."

"Dockins saved your life?" Jenny asked.

"Yeah," Chris said. He didn't offer an explanation, and nobody asked.

"Chris, are you sure you want to be the one to drop the hammer on him?" John asked.

"It has to be done," Chris said.

"I agree, but you don't have to be the one to do it," John said. "I can get someone else. Hell, I can do it."

"No," Chris said. "I have to be the one."

John looked at Don. "Don, feed everything you've got into your computer, then work up a most probable concept as to what our sniper is going to do next. I'm counting on you to give Chris all the support you can."

"All right," Don agreed.

John looked back at Chris. "Okay, it's your play, Chris. You're the point man."

"Thanks," Chris said.

First Lana, then Jenny hugged Chris. "I'm sorry you have to do this," Lana said.

Chris nodded.

On board the Delta flight to Mobile

"What would you like to drink, sir?" the flight attendant asked as the little cart approached his seat.

"Apple juice," Chris replied.

The flight attendant had a pleasant smile, but she was middle-aged and rather frumpy-looking. Chris could remember when they were called stewardesses, not flight attendants, and when they were all female, young, single, and pretty.

"Here you go, sir," she said, handing him the little plastic cup. Her smile was so pleasant and genuine that he regretted having made the unfavorable comparison.

Taking the glass, Chris tried to look through the window, but the Mobile flight was in one of the smaller Delta jets, and as Chris was a pretty good-sized man, the only thing he could see, without leaning over, was the clouds. He put his head back into the seat, listening to the whisper of the aft-mounted engines, and let himself be mesmerized by the cottony pillows of clouds.

November 22, 1990, the flight to Saudi Arabia

Sergeant Chris Farmer was looking through the window at the clouds. He was on a chartered flight filled with soldiers. Most were young and untried, but full of bravado. But many were quiet and reflective. These were the older soldiers, Vietnam veterans, who had been in combat before and knew what to expect.

One of the younger soldiers, with the rank of specialist, came up the aisle and squatted beside Chris's seat. He was holding a tablet on which several names were written.

"So, how about it, Sarge, you want in the pool?" he asked.

"What pool would that be, Dockins?"

"What pool? Why, *the* pool," Dockins answered. "The killing pool. It'll cost you fifty dollars to get in. So far we have ten people. The first one to bag a towel-head gets the money."

Chris shook his head. "No, I don't think so."

"Why not? Hell, you'll probably get the first one. I mean, you being the sergeant and all. You and Colonel Virden are tight, so he'll probably give you the first chance anyway. The truth is, you probably shouldn't be in the pool anyway. You've got an unfair advantage over all the rest of us."

"Don't you think there is something a little wrong about making up a pool on who kills the first man?"

"No, what's wrong with it?" Dockins asked. "I mean,

it's what we've been training for, isn't it? To kill the enemy. The way I look at it, it's like we've been coming out to basketball practice for all this time and now we are finally goin' to get in the game. Put me in, Coach, put me in. I'm ready," he said, laughing.

"Killing isn't a game, Dockins," Chris said. "It's serious business. And if you don't look at it that way, you could wind up getting yourself killed."

"So you say," Dockins replied. "But me? I'm going to get my jollies when I pop my first one."

"I'm sure you will," Chris said.

"So, what are you going to do? Puke when you shoot your first man? Come on, I mean, if you're all that queasy about it, why did you ever become a sniper in the first place? The way you're talking, I wonder if you'll even be able to do it."

"I can do it," Chris said.

"Yeah? Well, I'll bet you I do it first. Pool or not, what say me'n you just have us this little wager between us? Is it a bet?"

"Dockins, what's this I hear about a pool on who kills the first Iraqi?" a new voice asked.

Looking around, Dockins saw Colonel Virden standing in the aisle behind him. Colonel Virden was tall and muscular, with a well-trimmed mustache.

Dockins stood up. "It's just something for morale, Colonel," he said.

"Morale, huh?"

"Yes, sir."

"I don't like the idea of my men betting on who kills first. There will be no pools, do you understand? Give everyone their money back."

"Yes, sir."

"Sergeant Farmer, you weren't in this pool, were you?" Colonel Virden asked.

"No, sir," Chris answered resolutely.

Colonel Virden nodded. "Good man," he said.

Dockins slinked off to return the money, mumbling inaudibly to himself.

0630, January 17, 1991

The bombing of Baghdad had begun at 0300 that morning, but Sergeant Chris Farmer and five men of his target-interdiction squad were already fifty miles inside Iraq, having been put in by helicopter.

After a hike of some ten miles from the LZ, they reached their destination, an Iraqi outpost. Their target was Colonel Samir Ibrahim Abdullah. As chief of the death squad, Abdullah had executed several Kuwaitis before withdrawing to this particular outpost.

Chris's team consisted of three shooters and three spotters. Dockins was one of the shooters.

"Hey, Sarge, you got 'ny water left?" Dockins asked.

Chris glared at Dockins. "Have you drunk all your water already? Whatever happened to water discipline?"

"I don't have my canteen," Dockins said. "I took a drink on the chopper on the in. I must not've put it back right because it fell off. I think it's still on the helicopter." Dockins smiled at Chris. "Anyhow, you're our leader, so that means you have to look out for us, right? You aren't going to let me die of thirst."

"All right," Chris said, passing his canteen over.

Dockins took a long, Adam's-apple-bobbing drink, then passed the canteen back.

"We have a target," one of the spotters said.

"Is it Abdullah?" Chris asked, picking up a pair of binoculars to look in the same direction as his spotter.

"I don't know. It sure looks like him."

While Chris was looking through binoculars, Dockins took up a firing position. "Hey, Sarge, I've got him targeted," he said.

"Wait for a positive—"

Dockins's rifle boomed.

Chris had started to say wait for a positive ID, but before he could finish his sentence, Dockins had fired.

"I got his ass!" Dockins said excitedly.

"Wait! We've got movement!" the spotter said. "Sarge, Abdullah is coming out the back side of the bunker, headed for that Mercedes."

"Abdullah is coming out?" Dockins asked. "Then who the hell did I kill?"

"Probably some private," Chris said in disgust as, through his glasses, he watched the Mercedes pull away at top speed, leaving a rooster tail of dust climbing into the air behind it.

"We won't see that son of a bitch again," the spotter said, lowering his field glasses. "He's headed for Baghdad."

"You compromised our mission," Chris said to Dockins. "You should've waited for a positive ID."

"Hell, a dead Iraqi is a dead Iraqi," Dockins said. Then, suddenly, he shouted. "Sarge, look out!" Dockins pushed Chris down just as an RPG exploded near them. Had he not done so, Chris would've been killed.

"Sir? Sir?"

Looking around, Chris saw that the flight attendant was speaking to him.

Time and distance fell away, and he was no longer on the plane headed for Saudi Arabia. He was on the Delta flight bound for Mobile.

"I'm sorry," Chris said. "You said something?"

"I just asked for your empty glass," she said. The flight

attendant smiled. "I must say, though, you looked like you were a thousand miles from here."

"A lot more than a thousand miles, I'm afraid," Chris said. He handed his empty cup to the attendant. "How soon will we be landing in Mobile?"

"About twenty minutes," she answered. "Have you ever been to Mobile?"

"No."

"It's a beautiful city. I hope you have time to enjoy some of the sights."

"Thank you. I'll try," Chris said.

Shortly after landing, Chris went to the air-freight office. He stopped at the counter.

"Yes, sir?" the clerk said.

"Are you holding a package for John Teasdale?"

The clerk tapped a few keys on the computer. "Yes, we are," he said. "You're Teasdale?"

Chris showed him a Missouri driver's license and a military ID card indicating that he was a retired warrant officer. Both cards had been made up for him by Don Yee.

The clerk disappeared into the back for a moment, then came back out front, pushing a cart, on which there was a duffel bag.

"Heavy," the clerk said.

"Yes, it is. Thanks." Chris picked up the duffel bag without difficulty and took it out to his rental car. The bag contained Chris's PSG-1 sniper rifle, which was equipped not only with a scope, but with both a silencer and a flash suppressor. It also contained a sleeping bag, bottled water, and MREs. Everything he would need to maintain a position long enough for his quarry to show.

Ten

Chris Farmer met with his one-time commanding officer in a McDonald's restaurant on Airport Road. Chris thought the colonel looked old. The once-salt-and-pepper hair was now white, and he had added a beard to go with the mustache.

"The beard is a nice touch," Chris said with a smile as he dipped a French fry into the little cup of catsup.

"Thanks," Colonel Virden said. He stroked his beard. "I've always wanted one and used to envy the Navy because, from time to time, they would allow them. You're looking good. Civilian life agrees with you."

"Sometimes it does and sometimes it doesn't."

"Thanks for coming," Colonel Virden said. "This thing is . . . has gotten out of hand. Everyone is in a panic over it. And not just Mobile. It's spread all across the country."

"Do you know why he picked Mobile?"

"Yes, of course I do. He picked Mobile because of me, because of the court-martial."

"You mentioned the court-martial over the phone. That must've happened after I left the Army because I don't know anything about it."

"It was . . . uh . . . very personal," Colonel Virden said.

He took a drink before he continued. "Dockins raped my daughter, Chris."

"What? Why, that—"

Colonel Virden held out his hand to stop him. "To be honest, it was statutory rape only. My daughter was, well, I'll be generous and just say that she was going through a stage. Nevertheless, she was only fifteen. Dockins was almost ten years older, certainly old enough to bear the responsibility for his action. It happened back at Fort Bragg. They were in the backseat of a car out on Canopy Lane, and an MP caught them in the act."

"I'm sorry."

"Yes, well, I filed charges and Dockins got a DD. I think what is happening here is payback time."

"That might explain why he wants to make you feel guilty," Chris said. "But I believe you also said something about him killing for fun and profit?"

"Yes. He said that, and he said something else that was just as strange. He said he was on a holy mission."

"A holy mission?"

"Yes."

"I wonder what that was all about."

"Your guess is as good as mine," Colonel Virden said. "Chris, do you think you can get this guy?"

"I'll give it my best shot," Chris said.

Virden paused for a moment, then chuckled quietly. "Your best shot, huh? Well, you were the best I had, so I'd have to say that your best shot should be good enough. So, listen, are you going to stay with me while you are in Mobile? I run a very fine bed-and-breakfast."

"I can't, Colonel."

"It's Emile," Virden said.

Chris looked around the McDonald's. "I didn't choose this meeting place because of the cuisine. I chose it because there was less chance of our being seen together.

After this, we can't see each other again, or even talk to each other."

Colonel Virden nodded. "Yes, of course," he said. "I understand."

Chris put his hand across the table and squeezed the colonel's hand. "Have a good life, Emile."

"You too, Chris," Virden replied.

It had been a church once . . . twice actually. First it was St. Paul's Episcopal, then it was the African Brotherhood Powerhouse of God. Now it was an art gallery, part of the renovation of Mobile's historic Oakleigh District. Chris Farmer waited across the street from the old church in the loft of the Cotton Exchange.

Of course, the building where Chris was waiting was no more a cotton exchange now than the place across the street was a church. But it was still called the Cotton Exchange, even though it was the home of a little theater group. A marquee in front advertised *Cat on a Hot Tin Roof* as an upcoming production.

If the information supplied Chris by the Code Name Team was accurate, and he was certain that it was, he wouldn't have to wait long.

After John agreed that this was a mission worthy of the Code Name Team, Don Yee went to work, constructing a matrix of all the sniper's previous shootings. Feeding into the computer such considerations as length of shot, angle of shot, neighborhood composition, and all other variables, Don came up with a profile of the sniper, and a probability factor.

"Right here," Don said, pointing to a spot on the map. "The next shooting will take place right here."

"When?" Chris asked.

"I can't tell you exactly when," Don replied. "But my guess would be within three days."

"You're basing that on something, I suppose?"

"The longest separation between shootings has been fifty-seven hours. The shortest separation is twenty-four hours."

"All right," Chris said. "I'll buy that." He pointed to the spot on the map. "But what makes you so certain he will be here?"

"You think he is doing this to harass Colonel Virden?"

"Colonel Virden seems to think he is a central part of it, yes," Chris said. "Dockins has been calling him after every kill."

"Colonel Virden's house is right here," Don said, pointing to the map. "The sniper has already struck here, here, and here. And if you will notice, he is making a circle. This is the most logical place for him," Don said.

"All right. That sounds reasonable to me," Chris said.

"Also, on each of his previous shootings, the bullet has struck the victim from an angle no less than twenty-eight degrees, and no greater than forty degrees. In addition, every previous shooting has occurred at a significant intersection."

"What do you mean by significant?" Chris questioned.

"Significant in that it either has a good deal of foot traffic . . . or it is at a choke point in the neighborhood traffic flow."

Don picked up an oversized sandwich. In stature, Don was clearly the smallest member of the Code Name Team. Yet he could outeat any two of the other members, and his prodigious appetite was legendary.

He returned to the map. "There is an old church here," he said, or rather mumbled because his mouth was full of food. "That is, there is what used to be a church. I am told that it is now a gift shop or an art studio or something. Whatever it is now, the bell tower is still intact. And very near this old church is a significant intersection. A shot fired from the bell tower at anyone crossing that intersection would have a trajectory angle of thirty-seven degrees."

"So, you are telling me that our sniper is going to strike from there?" Chris asked.

"No, I'm not telling you that," Don said as he used his finger to poke a dangling piece of ham into his mouth.

"Well, if you aren't saying that, what has all this been about?"

"John told me to work up a 'most probable' concept," Don Yee said. "So that's what I've done."

"All right, if you were going to give it a score, how probable is this?" Chris asked.

Don Yee stuck the remainder of the sandwich into his mouth and chewed for a moment before he answered.

"I have given it a score," he replied as if wondering how Chris could even question it. "I would say that it has a probability factor of eighty-eight-point-six percent," he replied.

A probability factor of eighty-eight-point-six percent was convincing enough as far as Chris was concerned, so the first thing he did after arriving in Mobile was to stake out the old church. Finding the old Cotton Exchange just across the street was a fortunate break.

Chris looked over at his sleeping bag and water and food supply. He had been here for forty-eight hours now, staying completely out of sight. He had food and water enough to stay in position for another forty-eight hours, but he was hoping it wouldn't take that long.

Unscrewing the cap to one of the bottles of water,

Chris turned it up to his lips. The water was tepid and stale-tasting, and Chris had just taken a drink when he saw something across the street. It was a very subtle movement, little more than a shadow within a shadow, but Chris knew what it was. Putting his water bottle down, he picked up his PSG-1 rifle, got into position, and waited.

Dockins stayed low as he moved to the opening of the bell tower to have a look. Glancing toward the intersection, less that half a block away, he saw that he had the perfect shooting angle. Pleased with his choice, he opened his gun case and began assembling his rifle, fitting the pieces together with all the sensual pleasure of a man enjoying foreplay.

When his rifle was fully assembled, with the scope put in place, Dockins raised up again and looked down toward the intersection. He saw a heavy-set man with white hair and beard standing on the corner, waiting for the light to change. The man was wearing a cap and, through the scope, he could read the legend on the cap.

Vietnam Veteran, U.S. Army, the cap read.

"You picked a bad day to take a walk, my friend," Dockins said quietly. "You survived the jungles of Vietnam, only to be killed on a street corner in Mobile, Alabama. Ain't that a kick in the ass, though?"

Dockins stared through the scope, adjusting the focus and putting the crosshairs over the center of the Vietnam veteran's chest. His finger wrapped around the trigger and slowly began to tighten.

Across the street from the bell tower, in the loft of the Cotton Exchange, Chris Farmer had his own sight picture.

He put the crosshairs of his scope just over the end of the scope on Dockins's rifle. He caressed the trigger, and the rifle discharged, then rocked back against his shoulder.

Dockins felt the scope kick back against his face, but there was no time to assimilate that sensation before the bullet plunged through the scope, using his eye as an opening into his brain. The shock action of the bullet against his cerebral fluid caused enough hydrostatic pressure to blow out the back of his head. Rubin Dockins died without ever having the slightest idea of what had happened to him.

Because Chris had used both a flash suppressor and a silencer, people passed by on the sidewalk right underneath the Cotton Exchange with no idea of the drama that had just played out above them. At the intersection the light changed, and the white-haired, bearded Vietnam veteran crossed the street, totally unaware of his escape from death.

Chris gathered everything up, including the empty bottles and MRE packages, put everything in the duffel bag, then went down the service stairs to the rental car. One hour later the duffel bag was en route to Dallas, via air freight, and he was boarding the Delta flight back. Don Yee would meet him at the Addison airport and fly him back to Code Team Headquarters.

Within twenty-four hours the nation knew that the sniper had been killed. The rifle the police found with him was an exact ballistics match for the bullets they had taken from the victims, and on the floor beside him, there was the note, already written:"One shot, one kill."

Ironically, and the national news services made a great

deal out of this, it was evident that the sniper had been killed by a sniper. The mystery was, who did it? The FBI, police, and every other agency who had been working on the case denied that one of their snipers had pulled the trigger.

Morris called in Colonel Virden.

"Did you do it?" Morris asked.

"No. What makes you think I did it?"

"You told him he wouldn't get out of Mobile alive and he didn't. Also, he was obviously killed by a trained sniper. You were the head of the snipers."

"We call it target interdiction."

"Whatever you call it, did you do it?"

"I wish I was that good," Virden replied.

"Look. If you did do it, you did the world a favor. No charges will be filed. I just want to know the truth."

"I didn't do it," Colonel Virden said again.

Morris drummed his fingers on his desk for a moment as he studied Virden. Then he took a sharp breath. "I'll be damned," he said.

"What is it?"

"My dad was a captain during the Vietnam War. He went through OCS, and he told me that one of his instructors once asked him how to erect a fifty-foot flagpole. You know what the correct answer to that question was?"

Virden smiled. "I spent thirty years in the Army, Mr. Morris. Of course I know the correct answer to that question."

"The correct answer is, 'Sergeant, get that flagpole up,'" Morris said, ignoring the fact that Colonel Virden had said he knew the answer. "Did you do that, Colonel Virden? Did you say, 'Sergeant, get that flagpole up?'"

"You've seen my house, Agent Morris. You know I don't have a flagpole."

"And you know I'm not talking about a flagpole," Morris said. "That's what you did, isn't it? You set one of your own out to catch your own."

"If I did, do you really think I would tell you?" Virden asked.

"If you did," Morris said. He pointed at Colonel Virden. "If you did," he repeated. Then a slow smile spread across his face and, without a word, he saluted.

Colonel Virden returned the salute.

A few minutes later, he left the federal building and walked back down to his car. Just before he got into his car he paused for a moment.

"Sergeant," he said under his breath. "You put up a damn good flagpole."

Fountain Hills, Arizona

Bustamante was lying in a lounge chair on the deck of his swimming pool when Amber came out. She stood by the chair for a long moment, saying nothing.

"What is it?" Bustamante asked. He did not open his eyes. If he had, he would have seen that Amber was totally naked.

"I wonder if you would put some suntan oil on me," she said.

"Am I going to enjoy it?" he asked.

"You might enjoy it if you would open your eyes," Amber said.

Bustamante opened one eye and, seeing that she was naked, chuckled. "Yeah," he said. "I'll put some suntan oil on you. Afterward."

Amber turned to go back into the house.

"Where are you going?"

"I'm going back into the house."

"Why?"

"I thought you wanted to have sex."

"I do," Bustamante said. Standing, he stepped out of his swimming suit, revealing the fact that he was ready for her. "Right here."

"Pablo, no, not out here where everyone can see."

"Why should that make any difference to you? You used to fuck in porn movies, for crying out loud. Men and women."

"That was different."

"Yeah? What was different about it?"

"That was acting. I didn't feel anything for them."

"Ha! Like you feel something for me?"

"I do feel something for you," Amber insisted.

"I'm touched," Bustamante said flatly. "Come on."

"Where? Not on the concrete, I hope."

"On the lounge chair."

"The lounge chair won't hold us."

"It doesn't have to hold both of us. Just me."

"What do you mean?"

"All you need is a place for your knees," Bustamante said. He pointed to a rubber float. "Bring that over here. That'll do."

"You want a blow job out here?"

"Sure, why not?" Bustamante replied. "If the President can get a hummer in the Oval Office, I sure ought to be able to get one in the privacy of my own backyard." He smiled. "Just pretend there's a camera over there," he said. "And that ten million people are going to be beatin' off while they're watching."

"You are so romantic," Amber said sarcastically. She walked over to retrieve the rubber raft.

* * *

Bustamante was lying back in the chair, his hands were in Amber's hair, and Amber's head was in his crotch when the phone rang.

"Shit!" Bustamante said.

"Let it ring," Amber said, her voice muffled by her present circumstances.

"In my business, I can't afford to do that," Bustamante said, reaching for the phone.

Amber pulled away, but Bustamante pushed her head back into position. "No need for you to stop what you're doing," he said.

Amber resumed her activity.

"Yeah," Bustamante said.

"It's me, Todaro," the caller said.

"Yeah, Todaro, what is it?"

Smiling to herself, Amber increased the intensity, applying more pressure and using her tongue. She was determined not to be ignored during his telephone conversation, and her efforts paid off because she felt him grow tense.

"Oh, shit!" Bustamante said. "Shit, shit, shit, wait a—uhnnn . . . minute." His last words were barely audible as he let go.

"Pablo? Pablo, are you all right?" Todaro asked anxiously.

At the moment of his orgasm, Bustamante had put the phone down, and Amber could hear Todaro's voice. She picked up the phone and, smiling at Bustamante, handed it to him.

"Pablo, are you all right?" Todaro asked again.

"Yeah," Pablo said. "I'm fine. You just caught me at an awkward moment, that's all. What is it? What do you want?"

"Are you watching the news?"

"Am I watching the news? Hell, no, I'm not watching the news. You think I've got nothing better to do?"

"They got Dockins," Todaro said.

"Alive or dead?"

"Dead."

"That's good."

"Good?"

"Yes, it's good. Use your head. If he's dead, he can't tell them anything about us." He chuckled. "How many did he kill before they got him?"

"Nine."

"Then I'd say I got my money's worth, wouldn't you?"

"Yeah, if you put it that way, I guess you did," Todaro said. "Pablo, this makes up for what happened in New Orleans?" Todaro asked anxiously.

"It depends on how your other recruits do," Bustamante answered. "Tell Jubair it is his turn at bat."

"Will do," Todaro promised.

Hanging up the phone, Bustamante watched Amber go back into the house. He knew that Baldwin, and probably half of his household staff, had watched Amber go down on him. He found the thought arousing.

Moonlight Motel, Miami, Florida

Ly Kwan was sitting in the green, plastic-covered chair, watching a shopping channel on television. She had only been in the United States for six days, and she was amazed that so many wonderful things could be purchased just by watching TV.

Bill Smith, her husband of two days, came out of the bathroom, his hair still slightly damp from the shower.

"I've got to go out," he said.

"Shall I go with you?"

"Nah. Stay here and watch TV. I'll be back soon."

"Very well," Ly said. She pointed to the object being featured, a beautiful bracelet.

"I have never seen anything so beautiful," she said.

Bill laughed. "Ha!" he said. "It's as phony as a three-dollar bill."

"A three-dollar bill?" Ly asked, confused by the term.

"That means it isn't real."

"But how can they sell it if it isn't real?"

"How? They depend on dumb-assed people like you to buy their junk. That's how they stay in business."

Ly wasn't sure what dumb-assed meant, but she was certain it wasn't a complimentary term. Her face reflected her hurt feelings.

"Oh, don't get all bent out of shape," Bill said. "I didn't mean anything by it. You stay here and watch TV. When I come back, we'll go out for lunch."

"And can I have a hamburger?" Ly asked.

Bill laughed. "Yeah, you can have a hamburger."

Ly Kwan stared through the window as Bill drove away. Then she returned to the green plastic chair to watch television. There was a half-empty sack of potato chips on the table, and she reached for them. Until three days ago, she had never even seen a potato chip. What wonderful things they had in America!

Ly Kwan met her husband for the first time when she stepped off the plane less than a week ago. Their marriage had been arranged before she left China. This was the result of an ad she had answered, seeking foreign wives for American men.

Arranged marriages were not foreign to her culture, or to Ly Kwan's family. Her own parents had not met until the day they were wed. By marrying an American, Ly would acquire instant permanent residency status, and there were so many wonderful opportunities for her in America that her parents approved of her decision. This was even though they knew there was a possibility they would never see their daughter again.

As a young girl, Ly had been told that all Americans were rich, and since arriving in this country, everything she had seen so far seemed to validate that. Her husband had picked her up at the airport in his own car. In her village back in China, there were only three cars, and all three belonged to government officials.

A loud knock on the door interrupted her reverie, and thinking Bill had come back for her, she smiled happily and hurried to open the door. The smile was replaced by a look of curiosity when she saw two men standing there. She didn't know who they were, or what they wanted, but there was something about their countenance that frightened her. Before she could even question them, though, they pushed her back into the room, coming in after her and closing the door behind them. Both of them showed her badges.

"Who are you? What do you want?" she asked anxiously.

"You are Ly Kwan?"

"Yes."

"Ly Kwan, I am Agent Jones, this is Agent Black, we're with the immigration office," one of them said. "You are in this country illegally."

"No," Ly replied. "I have an entry visa. And now I am married to an American. That means I can stay here."

"We have no record of your being married," Agent Jones said.

"I have a paper that says—" Ly Kwan started, but she was interrupted.

"Come with us now. Don't give us any trouble," Agent Black said.

"But wait, my paper," Ly Kwan said, pointing toward

the dresser. "It is in the top drawer. Please let me get it so that I may prove I am married."

"I said come with us!" Black said again, more menacingly than before.

"What about my husband? He will wonder where I am."

Agent Jones put handcuffs on Ly. "You are under arrest," he said gruffly.

Ly was led out to the car. There were other residents of the motel standing around, watching in shock and curiosity as the beautiful young Chinese girl was forced unceremoniously into the car. Ly looked down in shame and embarrassment. She had never been in any difficulty with the authorities back home, but she knew people who had, and she knew that the best thing to do was to give them no trouble.

Ly was taken to a building downtown. There, with an American flag on the wall, and the sound of ringing phones, she was told to stand before the desk of another official-looking man.

"Ly Kwan, you have overstayed the length of your visa," the man said.

"No," Ly insisted. "I am married to an American. That means I can stay."

"Do you have proof that you are married?"

"I have papers back in the hotel, but the men who came for me would not let me get them."

"Very well, there is the telephone. You may call your husband."

Ly Kwan looked at the phone, then at the official. "I . . . I don't know how to call him," she said.

"Where is he?"

"I don't know."

"You say you are married, but you don't know where your husband is, and you don't know how to call him?"

Ly Kwan's eyes filled with tears, and one began sliding down her cheek. She shook her head.

"Doesn't he have a cell phone?"

"I don't know."

"You do see how it looks to us, don't you, Miss Kwan? You say you have a husband, but you don't know where he is, you don't know how to call him, and you don't know his cell phone number. You don't even know if he has a cell phone."

"No," Ly Kwan said quietly.

"You don't know, Miss Kwan, because you have no husband. This whole thing has just been a scam for you to get into the U.S."

"That's not true. I do have a husband."

"Maybe in the past you would have gotten away with something like this. But ever since the terror attacks of nine-eleven, our government has ordered us to crack down hard on illegal immigrants. I'm afraid you are going back to China," the man said.

"Please, come back to the hotel with me and wait until my husband returns. If I go back to China now, I will bring disgrace to myself and to my family."

"You should've thought of that before you tried to run this scam against the United States Government." He looked over at Agents Jones and Black, then made a nodding motion with his head. "Take this person away," he said. "Criminals like this sicken me."

"Come on, missy. We're going to the airport for a nice, long flight," Agent Black said.

Shortly after Ly Kwan left the office, another man came in from a back room. Smiling broadly, he reached out his hand.

"*Bill Smith* at your service," he said with a laugh, emphasizing the name Bill Smith.

"That was your wife?"

"She was my wife this week," he said. He handed over some papers. "Here is the marriage license she was wanting you to go back for."

The man behind the desk looked at it, then laughed. "United States Marriage License?" he said. "Aren't you taking sort of a chance there? What if you get some smart broad who knows that marriage licenses are issued only by the state?"

"If I did a state license, I could be found guilty of forgery," Bill Smith said. "Since there is no such thing as a United States Marriage License, I'm not forging anything."

"Yeah, I see what you mean. Nelson and Brewer are portraying 'Agents' Jones and Black with badges they bought from a theatrical costume shop." He opened the middle desk drawer and took out an envelope. "Okay, here's your money."

Bill Smith counted the money.

"It's all there, fifteen hundred dollars," the man behind the desk said.

"Yeah, I know. I just like to feel it, that's all. Fifteen hundred dollars for faking a marriage . . . plus three nights of some of the best ass I've ever had." He laughed out loud. "I love this job." He started toward the front door.

"Not that door, you idiot. She might still be out there. Use the back door."

"Yeah. Oh, and call me when the next one comes in. Maybe some hot Russian pussy."

"We'll keep in touch," the man behind the desk promised.

Eleven

Having completed his ablutions, Cesar Adib Jubair stood in the mosque, preparing to offer his morning prayers.

"I intend to offer this Salat Fajr for Allah. *Allah u Al-kaber.* Allah is great. In the name of Allah. I depend on Allah. There is no ability or power except by the leave of Allah.

"*Bismillahi tawakkaltu alal-lah. La Haola Wala Qowwata illa Billah.*

"*Bismillah I rrahman I erraheem. Al humdo lil-lahi rab-bil al ala-meen. Arrahman I rraheem. Maliki yaum I eddeen. Iyyaka nabudu wa iyyaka nasta een. Ihdinas sirata almus-taqeem. Siratal lazhina anamta alaihim, ghairil maghdubi alaihim, wa la adhdhaal leen.*

"Grant me the strength to commit martyrdom so that, in giving my own life, I will take the lives of infidels who do not honor you."

While he was in the mosque, surrounded by other Muslims and the trappings of his faith, Jubair's blood ran hot with hatred for the infidels, and his heart was strong with the determination to enter into paradise through the means of martyrdom.

With the spiritual preparations made, Jubair returned to his apartment, a third-floor walk-up on Clark, to make the physical preparations. Very carefully opening the box he had taken from Unit 271 at the Lincoln Storage Company, he used the components therein to assemble the bomb he would need. As he worked, the television played in the background.

"Come on down to Mitchell Sharp Lincoln-Mercury and let us put you in a new car. You have never experienced luxury until you have slipped behind the wheel of the elegant Town Car," the announcer was saying.

Jubair looked at the car in the picture. A man was escorting a beautiful blond woman to the car. Opening the door, he helped her in, then moved around to the driver's side, got behind the wheel, and drove away.

Jubair walked over to the window and looked down onto the street at his own car, a 1993 Ford Taurus. The right rear window was covered over with cardboard and duct tape, and the left rear door was a different color from the rest of the car.

He remembered how proud he had been of the car when he first bought it. It was the first car he had ever owned, and it had served him well, but it would be nice to drive a Lincoln like the one in the TV commercial. And with the money he was promised for setting off the bomb, he could do it.

He looked back toward the fuse and timer of the incomplete bomb. If he carried through with his vow for martyrdom, he wouldn't need the Lincoln, or the money. In fact, in his suicide note, he had written that the money was to be given to Mindanao Muslim Front.

On the other hand, the bomb would still have the same effect whether he died in the blast or not. And martyrdom was forever, which meant it had no clock. He could become a martyr now, or he could become one later.

Jubair returned to the bomb. He would have to redo the fuse. Instead of setting it off manually, he would do it by remote.

What if the bomb went off while he was preparing it? That had happened before, many times. He knew of warriors who were killed when the bomb they were making exploded.

So be it. If Allah chose to grant him instant martyrdom, then he would enter paradise with a smile on his lips. *Allah u Al-kaber.*

Zabakabad, Sitarkistan

When the plane touched down, Ly Kwan looked out the window and was surprised to see that the signs were written, not in the familiar Chinese characters, but in Arabic and English.

WELCOME TO ZABAKABAD, SITARKISTAN, a large sign read.

Ly turned to Agent Black. "I don't understand," she said. "Where are we?"

"Like the sign out there says, honey, we're in Sitarkistan," Agent Black answered.

"But I thought I was being sent back to China."

"Do you think China would want you now?"

"But China is my home."

The man shook his head. "No. China was your home. You gave it up when you came to the United States."

"Yes, to marry an American," Ly Kwan said.

"We checked your records. You are not married to an American."

"Yes, I am," Ly Kwan insisted. "And if you had given

me time to prove it, I would have shown you the marriage license. But you took me away before I could do so. I couldn't even call my husband to tell him where I was," she said, her eyes welling with tears.

"Tell her, Nelson."

"What?"

"Tell her the truth. It can't hurt anything now."

"The truth?" Ly asked.

"Tell her."

Nelson sighed. "Honey, I'm not Agent Jones, and he isn't Agent Black. My name is Nelson, he's Brewer."

"And we aren't immigration agents," Brewer said.

"If you aren't immigration agents, then why did you take me from my husband?"

"And he isn't your husband," Brewer continued.

"Yes, he is. I told you, I have—"

"A marriage license, I know," Brewer said. "But it is as phony as Bill Smith is."

"Phony? What is phony?"

"Fake. Not real. You never were married. It was just a way to get you to come to America."

"But why did you want me to come to America, and then you take me away from America?"

"Business," Nelson said. "Nothing personal, you understand. It's just business."

They left the airport in an ancient and rattling yellow-and-blue Citroen taxicab. The street was filled with vehicles, from expensive cars to old trucks that looked as if they were barely staying together, to ox-drawn carts, to camels. The buildings of the city were as eclectic as the traffic in the street. Some were quite modern-looking; others looked like little more than mud huts. She was surprised to see that one of the more modern of the buildings was displaying an American flag. As they drove by she saw by the sign out front, that it was an American embassy.

After a drive of some twenty minutes, they stopped in front of a three-story building in the middle of the block. The two men she had thought of as Agents Black and Jones, but now knew to be Brewer and Nelson, took her, not through the front door, but up a set of stairs that climbed the side of the building.

"In there," Nelson said as he pushed open the door.

A short, swarthy man with a beard and dressed in Arab clothing met them inside. He stared at Ly with eyes that, though very dark, seemed to have tiny red lanterns glowing at the bottom.

"Very nice," he said. Reaching out, he grabbed her breast and squeezed. The move was so unexpected that Ly made no effort to avoid him, and she was shocked when she felt his fingers caress her nipple.

"Yes, yes, very nice," the man said.

"You have the money?" Brewer asked.

"Twenty-five thousand dollars American, just as we agreed." The Arab opened a drawer on the file cabinet and took out a leather case. Opening the case, he dumped the money on the top of his desk. "Do you care to count it?"

"Nah. I trust you," Nelson said. "Because I know that you know what will happen to you if you try to short-change Mr. Bustamante." Nelson laughed, then nodded toward Ly Kwan. "She's all yours now. You be a good girl, Miss Kwan, and do exactly what he tells you, and you'll be all right."

Ly Kwan was now more confused than ever. First, she had thought she was being deported to China, only to find herself in Sitarkistan. Then she'd learned that the two men who had taken her weren't who they told her they were, and weren't even officials of the government. Now they were leaving her in a strange city with a strange man.

"My name is Massur," the Arab said.

"Mr. Massur, I don't understand—" Ly began, but her sentence was interrupted when Massur slapped her in the face, very hard.

Ly gasped in pain, then put her hand to her face and looked at Massur through frightened eyes.

"Woman, you must learn to speak only when you are invited to speak," Massur said.

"But who are you? Why am I—"

Massur slapped her again, as hard this time as he did the first time.

"Are you a slow learner? Speak only when you are invited to speak."

Ly Kwan's cheek felt as if it were on fire and she had a ringing in her ears. Tears began flowing down her face, but she took care not to sob aloud, lest it be taken as talking.

"That's better," Massur said. "You may ask one question.

"Why am I here?" Ly Kwan asked.

"You are here because you belong to me," Massur said. "You are my slave to do with as I please. I paid twenty-five thousand dollars in American money for you and you will not leave here until you have paid me back. Do you know how you are going to do that?"

Ly shook her head no, but said nothing.

"Good, very good. You are learning. You will pay me back by providing sexual services for me, and for anyone that I tell you to. And you will do it gladly." He pushed a button on his desk, and a moment later another woman appeared.

"This is Ly Kwan. Take her into the back and introduce her to the others," Massur said.

"Ly Kwan? What a lovely name. My name is Brenda. Come with me, dear."

Ly followed Brenda down a long hallway.

"I'll put some ice on that face. That will ease the pain and help with the swelling, but it won't stop the bruise, I'm afraid."

Ly said nothing.

"Oh, my dear, you can talk to me, or to any of the others," Brenda explained. "It is only Mr. Massur who has such strict rules."

"Is Mr. Massur your husband?" Ly asked.

Brenda laughed. "No, nothing like that," she said. "I came here the same way you did. I left Britain, thinking I was going to marry a very wealthy sultan. At least, that's what I was told."

"So, you are a slave too?"

"Well, not quite a slave," Brenda admitted. "I suppose I could leave if I wanted to, but Mr. Massur has made it very profitable for me to stay here. Besides, where would I go? Back in Britain I would be just another whore. And to be honest with you, dear, I'm a little too old now for that. In here."

Brenda led Ly through a pair of double doors into a large room. Here, Ly saw several other women, and she gasped when she saw how provocatively they were dressed, or undressed, for at least three of them were totally naked.

"This is the room where we meet the gentlemen callers," Brenda said.

"Who are all these girls?" Ly asked.

"Like you, they are white slaves."

"White slaves?" Ly Kwan asked. Two of the girls were black, and she looked at them.

Brenda chuckled. "The fact that we are called white slaves has nothing to do with the color of our skin," she explained. "White slavery is what they call the business of buying and selling women for sexual purposes. You exist now solely to provide sexual pleasure for men."

"How long?" Ly Kwan asked.

"How long?"

"Mr. Massur said I would be here until I paid him back. How long does that take?"

Some of the other girls laughed.

"What is so funny?"

"That is just something he says to all the girls when they arrive. You will never work your way out of here."

"Oh," Ly said.

"Come, my dear, I'll show you your room. It's really quite nice, considering," Brenda said. "And though it is small, you will have it all to yourself. That is the one advantage we all have to being in the business of providing sexual services. You see, most of our clients are very shy about such things, and they wouldn't want anyone to see them in such compromising situations."

Chicago, Illinois

When the ancient Ford Taurus stopped in the middle of the intersection, Cesar Adib Jubair got out, lifted the hood, and stared for a moment at the engine. Reaching down inside, he made some sort of adjustment.

Other cars approaching the intersection were forced to stop and, for a moment, they sat there quietly, feeling some sense of sympathy for the hapless driver. Jubair was counting on that innate courtesy to give him the time he needed to arm the bomb. That task accomplished, he slammed his hood. Then, to the surprise of the many gathered drivers, he didn't get back into his own car. Instead, he started walking away.

A cabbie rolled down his window, then leaned out of his car. "Hey, wait a minute! What are you doin'?" he shouted. "You can't leave that piece of shit there!"

Jubair began to run.

"Hey, what's goin' on here?" the cabbie shouted again.

By now, traffic was beginning to back up, and some of the cars started honking impatiently. A bus, filled with people, had just stopped at the bus stop and it was blocked there, unable to pull away from the curb.

Two men got out of their cars and started toward the stalled car. The cabbie and one more man got out to join them. The cabbie opened the door and grabbed the steering wheel, while the others began pushing from behind.

Suddenly the car erupted in a large, whooshing ball of flame. The concussion of the explosion was felt a block away, and when the fireball disappeared and the smoke rolled away, the four men who were trying to push the car out of the intersection now lay dying or dead in the street. In addition, there were more dead and dying in the bus, which had received the brunt of the explosion.

People left their cars, some to offer help to the wounded, but many to run away in fear. A few just wandered around in shock, as if they were unsure of where they were.

As it happened, a remote TV truck was only seven cars back from the intersection when the explosion happened. A cameraman and a reporter ran from the truck to the scene. The reporter was on his cell phone.

"We've just had an explosion at the intersection of State and East Grand! Get me a live feed!"

* * *

Code Name Team Headquarters

John and the others were watching television as the newscaster, in breathless tones, told of the blast that he had witnessed.

"We were the seventh car back," the newscaster said, speaking earnestly into a handheld mike, "and though our vehicle wasn't damaged, every car in front of us was, including a bus, which was totally destroyed.

"There are no complete numbers as yet on how many were killed, but because the loaded bus was at the stop at the point of the explosion, the casualty count will likely be quite high."

The picture showed a blackened bus, with all the windows blown out. Then the camera found a small, stuffed bear on the ground by the bus, and it focused on the bear for a long, telling moment.

"So far twelve have been reported killed and many more wounded," the newscaster continued. "The police have no clues as to motive, nor as to who might have planted the bomb, but we do know that it was a bomb, and not an accidental explosion."

John picked up the remote and turned the picture off. "What do you think?" he asked the others.

"Clearly terrorists," Mike said.

"Yes, but who? Middle-Eastern? Or home-grown?"

"Home-grown? What, you mean you think an American could do something like that?" Mike asked.

"Does the name Timothy McVeigh mean anything to you?" Jennifer asked.

"Oh, yeah," Mike agreed. "I guess you're right."

* * *

John was walking deliberately through the small town, pistol in hand, his eyes sweeping back and forth, checking the windows, doors, and roofs of the buildings that lined either side of the street. Suddenly a man popped up in the upper window of the house to his left while, at almost the same time, another target presented itself in the doorway of a house to his right.

John fired to his left first, hitting his target right between the eyes. Swinging to his right, he sent two bullets into the target's heart. Another door popped open and John swung his pistol to engage, but saw that it was a woman, carrying a bag of groceries. He lowered his pistol, but suddenly the woman dropped the groceries, and John saw that she was holding an AK-47. He fired quickly, hitting her in the middle of the head.

"Very good, very good," Don said, clapping his hands behind him. John began loading his pistol, as all the targets were reset.

"Hello, Don," John said as he pushed new bullets into the empty magazine. "What brings you to Dry Gulch City? Surely you aren't going to take a round of target practice, are you?"

Don held up his hands. "No, no, not me. Fieldwork is for you heroes. My job is in the computer room."

"Yes, but a little target practice now and then wouldn't hurt you."

"Maybe. But if I had been out here wasting time with you, I wouldn't have come up with this, would I?" He showed John a sheet of paper.

"What is it?"

"The feds have identified the Chicago bomber by his car," Don said. "His name is Cesar Adib Jubair."

"Jubair? Hmm, it doesn't ring a bell. Is he an Arab terrorist?"

"Not Arab. Filipino," Don answered. "But I've just come up with something very, very interesting."

"Oh? What?"

"Three days before the bombing, there was an electronic transfer of one hundred thousand dollars to Jubair's bank account."

"That's interesting," John said.

"Yes, especially since three days before the first sniper shooting in Mobile, there was an electronic transfer of one hundred thousand dollars to Rubin Dockins's account."

John was just sliding the last bullet into the magazine, and when Don said that, he looked up sharply.

"The hell you say."

"The hell I do say," Don said.

"Now, that is very interesting. What do you think the odds of something like that would be?"

"One hundred sixty-two million to one," Don answered.

John chuckled. "I should know better than to ever ask rhetorical questions around you."

"I'm going to ask Wagner to—" That was as far as Don got before John suddenly shot at him, or at least at his feet. "What the hell!" Don shouted, dancing back from the drifting puff of dust the impact of the bullet had raised.

John nodded toward the ground beside Don and there, writhing in its death throes, was a rather large rattlesnake.

"He was showing a real interest in those snakeskin boots you're wearing," John said with a chuckle. "I don't know if the boots were his mother, or if he had just suddenly fallen in love with them."

"You scared the shit out of me, man!" Don said.

"Which would you rather be? Scared? Or bitten?"

"All right, all right, scared," Don said as he walked

away. "But don't expect me to thank you," he shouted back over his shoulder.

The next afternoon John was in the gym, in a full-contact karate match with Linda. Linda was good, damn good, and though John could generally beat her, he had to be on his toes at all times to do it.

"John, I've got something!" Don shouted, coming toward him.

John looked toward Don and when he did, Linda swept her leg around, catching him at the bend of his knees and bringing him down. She moved quickly to take advantage, sending a swift kick toward his crotch, stopping it at the very last minute and smiling down at him.

"Gotcha," she said.

"Damn," John said, getting back to his feet. "Did you pay him to come in here?"

"Nope," Linda replied. "But I do know how to keep my mind on my business."

"Yeah, well, I'll give you that. Oh, and thanks for not making me a soprano."

Linda laughed. "My pleasure," she said.

"Did I come at a bad time?" Don asked.

"No, I get my ass kicked every now and then, just to stay humble," John replied. He reached for a towel and began drying the sweat from his face. "What have you got?"

"Another one hundred thousand dollars just showed up in Jubair's bank account," Don said.

"How? I thought the police were looking for him."

"They are. But like the first one, this was an electronic transfer."

"It was? Well, can you tell where it came from?"

"I traced it back through six accounts, then hit a firewall," Don said. "If I keep working on it, I'm sure I'll crack it eventually. But right now I have no idea where it's coming from."

"I wonder what the deposit means," John said.

"If you ask me, it's payment for the job he did."

"You mean you think he was hired to do the bombing?"

"Yes. Just like Dockins was hired to shoot a few people down in Mobile."

"Yes," John said. He stroked his chin as he looked at the paper Don handed him. The paper detailed Don's search for the origin of the money. "I agree with you. I believe he was hired to do the bombing. But I disagree that this second transfer was payment for the job already done."

"Well, what do you think it is?"

"I think it's payment for a job he's going to do."

"Another bombing?"

"It could be."

"Where?"

"I wish I knew the answer to that."

St. Louis, Missouri

When the security guard saw the man leaving the back entrance of the neighborhood medical clinic, he called out to him.

"Hey! What are you doing back there? You aren't supposed to be back there."

The man made no answer.

"What are you doing back here?"

There was still no answer.

"Come here!" the security guard called, pulling his radio up to call for assistance.

"God is great!" Cesar Adib Jubair shouted. There was a smile on his face as he set off the bomb that killed himself, the security guard, and seven others.

Twelve

Zibakabad, Sitarkistan

Before he left Sitarkistan, Pablo Bustamante had provided Jahmshidi Mehdi with a contact who could, in Bustamante's words, "provide beautiful and willing women to fulfill your wildest dreams."

Although he took the information from Bustamante, Jahmshidi had no intention of following through with it. As it was, he felt flushed with guilt over his sexual indulgences with the women on board Bustamante's plane. After a few days, though, the feeling of guilt was replaced by his memories of exquisite pleasure, along with a desire to experience such delight again.

Jahmshidi fought with his conscience. He knew that such activity was sinful and he would be putting his soul at risk if he repeated it. On the other hand, he knew also that one of the rewards for martyrdom and faithfulness would be a harem of seventy-two virgins provided for him the moment he arrived in paradise.

That being the case, why would it not be acceptable for someone who was truly a warrior for Allah, someone who was a defender of the faith, and who would willingly give his life for Islam, to enjoy an earthly sample? After all, he was not an ordinary person. He was a dedicated martyr.

Convinced that what he was doing would be acceptable in the eyes of Allah, Jahmshidi Mehdi called the number Bustamante gave him.

"You understand that this is very expensive," the contact told him.

Money was no object to Jahmshidi; he had hundreds of thousands of dollars at his disposal, contributions from supporters all over the world. Of course, some contributed money thinking it was to help to feed and house the poor. Others thought it would help in defending the faith, while many realized that it would be spent in conducting terrorist operations. But no one believed that it would be used to pay for Jahmshidi's sexual pleasure.

"I have money," Jahmshidi replied. His tongue was so thick that he was having trouble making it work, and his mouth was dry with a desire that was now maddening his senses.

The contact gave him an address. "Bring one thousand dollars," Jahmshidi was told.

The sign in front of the building said that it was an international men's business club, and Jahmshidi had to pay a stiff membership fee in order to gain entry. Just inside the front door was a large lobby. The lobby was furnished with leather chairs and sofas, coffee tables and end tables, and well-stocked bookshelves. A dozen men sat on chairs or the sofas, reading and drinking coffee that was served to them by young men dressed in white.

For a moment, Jahmshidi thought he had made a mistake, for there were no women in sight. Then one of the club's staff members approached him.

"May I help you?"

"Yes, I . . . uh." Jahmshidi did not know how to ask for what he really wanted, but the one who greeted him was an astute observer of human behavior and realized at once, from Jahmshidi's embarrassed demeanor, what he was after.

"If you would come this way, sir," he said, leading Jahmshidi toward the back of the room. There appeared to be no openings in the panel wall, but when they got there, the staff member moved one of the geometric pieces in the fret and a panel slid open.

The host led Jahmshidi through the opening, down a hallway, and into another room, rather like the one out front, though not quite as large.

"If you will wait here for a moment," he was told. Then the man withdrew, leaving Jahmshidi alone.

Jahmshidi looked around the room at the lush furnishings and expensive appointments. A Tabriz rug covered the decorative tile floor.

From the back of the room another panel slid open, and a man wearing Arab dress came in.

"I am Massur," the man said amiably. "Do you have the one thousand dollars?"

"Yes," Jahmshidi said. "I have the one thousand dollars." He removed the money from his billfold and handed it to Massur.

Massur counted the money, then folded it over and put it in a golden money clip. "Come with me."

Following Massur through a panel opening at the back of the room, Jahmshidi felt as if he had truly exited one world and entered another. Behind him the leather and wood-paneled parlor was very much like the one out front, where men sat drinking coffee or tea, reading and meditating.

On this side of the panel, however, everything changed. The air was filled with music and scented with some sort of stimulating incense. A very pretty young woman approached him, carrying a tray. A glass of wine sat on the tray and, smiling, the woman extended the glass to Jahmshidi.

"No, I, uh, don't drink," Jahmshidi replied, trying to put the wine back on the little tray the woman was carrying.

"My friend, do you not know that wine will be served in paradise?" Massur asked.

"Yes, I know that."

"Then perhaps you should learn to drink it here, on earth, so you will not be considered an ingrate when it is offered to you there."

"Yes," Jahmshidi agreed. "Yes, that is true, isn't it?" He took the glass and drank it, enjoying the taste and sensation of the controlled fire of the fruit on his tongue.

"Come, I will lead you to the place where you can make your selection," Massur said.

Taking a second goblet of wine with him, Jahmshidi followed Massur into another room. As soon as he stepped through the door, he gasped for breath. There were at least thirty women in this room in various stages of undress, from transparent lingerie, to complete nudity. Jahmshidi experienced an immediate erection, the palms of his hands grew sweaty, and he felt dizzy.

"As you can see, we have women from all over the world," Massur said.

"Why no Sitarkistanian women?" Jahmshidi asked as he looked at what could have been King Solomon's harem.

"Would you want our women defiled so that they could not enter into paradise?" Massur asked.

"No, of course not."

"Nor would I. That is why we use only infidel women."

"How do you get them to come to Sitarkistan?"

"As we provide the women for your pleasure, we have a service that provides the women to us."

"Are any of the women from America?"

"Yes," Massur replied. "Many are from America."

"I would not think that American women would want to come to such a place It is said that, in America, they are treated just as the men are treated."

"Yes, this is true," Massur said. "But many American women are addicted to drugs and alcohol, and that makes it easy for us to recruit them."

"What about that one?" Jahmshidi asked, pointing to a beautiful, almond-eyed girl. "She looks Oriental."

"Yes, a Chinese girl. She has only recently arrived, but I think you will be pleased with her. Would you like to sample the delights she has to offer? She is not only beautiful, she is really quite skilled in the art of pleasing men."

"Yes," Jahmshidi said. "I want her."

Massur pointed at the girl Jahmshidi chose, and with her face devoid of any expression whatsoever, the young Chinese girl rose from the silk pillow where she had been sitting and came toward them. Her walk and movements were so smooth and fluid that Jahmshidi got the impression that she was gliding toward him, instead of walking. The girl's sloe eyes flashed blackly, and her golden skin shone softly in the subdued lighting.

"You have made a good choice, my friend," Massur said.

"What will she do for me?" Jahmshidi asked.

"Anything you ask of her," Massur replied. "She is not allowed to refuse any request from our important guests." Massur smiled obsequiously. "You are one of the more important of our guests," he added.

"Will she do all this for the one thousand dollars? Or will she ask for more?"

"Oh, the money is not for her," Massur explained.

"Don't you understand? She has no choice but to do what I tell her to do. She is a slave."

"What is your name?" Jahmshidi asked. The woman glanced toward Massur.

"You may answer him," Massur said.

"My name is Ly Kwan," Ly said.

"Are you Muslim, Ly Kwan?"

"No."

"Good," Jahmshidi replied. "I would not want to be responsible for the eternal damnation of a Muslim. Even a female."

"I am sure that Allah is pleased with your piety," Massur said.

"Where do we go?" Jahmshidi asked.

"She will lead you," Massur said, nodding toward Ly Kwan.

Nodding, Ly turned and started out of the room with Jahmshidi following close behind.

Jahmshidi was not the first "guest" Ly Kwan had entertained, and she had learned how to take her soul from her body, how to set all emotions and feelings aside. She began removing her clothes, not even aware of Jahmshidi's lustful gaze.

Fountain Hills, Arizona

Amber D'Amour was standing just outside the living room, listening to Pablo talking on the phone.

"What's the new crop like?" he asked.

She couldn't hear the answer.

"Really?" He laughed. "Well, maybe that's the reason they're all answering the ads to come to the States to marry Americans. Maybe they are such dogs that they can't find anyone to marry them in their own country."

Again, she couldn't hear the response, but again, Pablo laughed.

"Tell you what. Next time we get a really good-looking woman in, bring her out here. I'll 'marry' her for a while. What? Yeah, well, you let me worry about Amber. Hell, that bitch stays so spaced out all the time she won't even notice."

Amber felt tears sliding down her cheeks.

"Yeah, I agree. She was a looker when I first brought her out here. But the stuff is getting to her, man. I'm going to have to find some way to get rid of her."

Amber turned and hurried back to her room. She accidentally kicked a table in the hallway, causing a vase to fall to the floor and break. She gasped as she looked at the bright blue shards on the floor.

Baldwin heard the vase fall and came to check on it. Seeing the horrified look on Amber's face, he tried to put her at ease.

"Don't worry about it, Miss D'Amour," he said. "It's not one of the more expensive ones." He started to pick up the pieces.

"Leave it," Pablo said from the far end of the hall. "I don't pay you all that money to clean this pig's mess up. Go get one of the maids."

"All right," Baldwin said. He went after a maid, leaving just Pablo and Amber in the hall. Pablo stared at Amber with such intensity that she couldn't meet his gaze and she started looking at the floor.

"Were you listening in?" he asked.

"No."

"Don't lie to me, bitch."

"I . . . I heard only your side of the conversation. By accident," Amber said. "I wasn't listening in."

"I want you out of here."

"No," she gasped. "No, Pablo, please! Where would I go?"

"I don't give a shit where you go, or what you do. You can die, as far as I'm concerned. You're nothing but a worthless doper."

"That's funny, coming from you. You've made all your money dealing in dope."

"Yeah, well, there's a reason they call it dope, you know. Because it's for dopes. I might sell it, but I've never been so stupid as to use it. What the hell happened to you? You were a looker when I brought you here. Now look at you."

"Maybe if you had paid more attention to me, I wouldn't have had to become a user."

"That's bullshit and you know it. I've got some business to take care of. When I come back, I want your ass out of here."

When Baldwin returned with one of the maids, Amber went into her room and slammed the door. She paced nervously back and forth in her room for a few minutes. She felt like she was coming apart, like a dandelion being scattered in the wind.

Suddenly she had the panicky thought that Pablo might have come into her room, might have gotten into her stash. Opening her jewelry box, she lifted out the tray and looked down inside, then breathed a sigh of relief. It was there. Everything she needed was there.

She took out the band, tied it around her arm to cause the vein to protrude, then shot up. Within seconds she felt the anxiety fall away. She could almost picture the little airborne seeds of the dandelion plant coming together again. She was bathed in euphoria.

Relaxed now, she lay on her bed.

"Fuck Pablo," she said aloud.

She giggled, then wagged her finger back and forth.

"That's what I was going to do, but he doesn't want it, so if he doesn't want me to fuck him, fuck him."

She laughed out loud.

"Fuck him if he doesn't want to be fucked," she said again.

She could be a comedy writer. That was the funniest line she had ever heard. She could be a stand-up comedienne on the Comedy Channel delivering that line.

"So I said to him, if you don't want me to fuck you, fuck you."

She laughed again.

Then she got an idea. She knew how she could get back in Pablo's good graces. She had overheard enough of his conversations to know that he was engaged in committing acts of terror as payment for his product. She knew also that he was paying a lot of money to the people who were carrying out the acts for him.

"That's what I'll do," she said aloud. "I'll make the biggest splash yet, and I won't charge him a dime."

It was a two-day drive from Fountain Hills, Arizona to Dallas, Texas. Amber had to drive because she would never be able to get on a plane carrying the C-4 explosive she had in the backseat of the car.

She made it to Van Horn, Texas, the first night, staying in the Star Light Motel. The night clerk, a skinny, pimply-faced young man in his mid-twenties, had three earrings in his right ear and spiderweb tattoos on each of his shoulders. He wore thick glasses and had a prominent Adam's apple.

Amber could feel him staring hard at her as she registered. He gave her the key to her unit, then grabbed the card and looked at it.

"I'll be damned!" he said aloud. "It *is* you!"

"I beg your pardon?"

"Hold it," the clerk said. "Wait right there."

Amber panicked for a moment. Did he know she had C-4 in her car? Was there a police bulletin out for her?

The clerk opened a cabinet and moved some boxes aside, then came up with an encased videotape. "This here is *Muff-diving Muppet*," he said, holding it toward her. You're the star in it, ain't you?"

So relieved was Amber that she wasn't being sought by the police that she smiled broadly and nodded. "Yes," she said. "Yes, that's me."

"Damn it! I knew it!" the night clerk said. He held the box out toward her. "Would you autograph this for me? I ain't never met no one famous before."

"Of course I'll autograph it," Amber said, returning, with some relief, to the counter. She picked up the pen and signed her name on the box.

"Goddamn," the clerk said, looking at her autograph. "Goddamn, goddamn, goddamn! Ain't this somethin', though? I'm goin' to remember this night."

Amber got an idea. She was tired and strung out. Maybe a little diversion would be good for her.

"How would you like to do something that would really make you remember this night?" she asked.

"What?" the clerk replied.

"Did you like the movie *Muff-diving Muppet*?" Amber asked.

"Are you kiddin'? I've seen it so many times I've near 'bout wore it out."

"How would you like to come to my room and act that movie out?" Amber asked.

"How we goin' to do that?" the clerk asked. "That movie was of you and some other woman goin' down on each other. We don't have another woman."

"We don't need one, do we?" Amber replied. "I do have a muff. And you do have a tongue."

The clerk looked confused for just a second; then he realized what she said.

"Goddamn! You want me to go down on you, don't you?"

"That's the general idea."

"Yeah! Yeah! Son of a bitch! Yeah!" the clerk said. "Let me close and lock up."

The clerk locked the door to the office, then pointed to the room that was to be Amber's room. "You can just park your car down there," he said.

"Thanks," Amber replied, crawling into her car.

"Wow, this here is a Beamer, ain't it?" the night clerk said, looking at her BMW sports convertible.

"Yes."

"Well, yeah, sure, I mean, you bein' a famous movie star 'n all, you'd be drivin' somethin' like this. Oh, I was about to ask what you was doin' in a town like Van Horn, but I see you got a present already wrapped. You goin' somewhere for Christmas?"

"Yes."

The clerk reached for it. "What'd you get? I've always wondered what rich and famous people bought for Christmas presents."

"Nothing special," Amber replied, moving the box out of his reach. "Look, if you're just going to stay out here and gab all night, maybe we'd just better call everything off."

"No, no!" the clerk said. "I was just bein' friendly is all." He pointed to the unit she had just rented. "I'll meet you down there," he said.

Thirteen

Don Yee was eating *chow mai fun,* his chopsticks snapping open and closed over the take-out box as he studied the program on the computer monitor. Numbers were flashing by so quickly that he couldn't read them.

The program Don had running was comparing the filtrate signatures from the powder residue of various explosions. He had just received, through personal contact, samples from the bomb blasts in Chicago and St. Louis. He was running those against the signatures he already had embedded within the program, including the blast that destroyed the Murrah Federal Building in Oklahoma City, the one at the Atlanta Olympics, the first WTC bombing, the bombs of the Unabomber, Ted Kaczynski, and half a dozen others.

Suddenly the program stopped, and the word "Match" appeared on the screen.

"Ah-ha!" Don said, spraying little bits of pork in his exuberance.

The screen went black for a second, and when it came up, there were three matches, not just the two that Don was looking for.

"Well, now, hello here," Don said, looking up at the screen. "Three matches?"

He typed in the three sets of numbers, then hit enter. After a moment, the results of his matching search hit the screen.

1. Dempsey's Warehouse explosion, Miami, Florida, August 21, 2002.
2. Chicago intersection explosion, December 5, current year.
3. St. Louis Medical Clinic explosion, December 12, current year.

Don went on-line to a search engine and typed in the words "Dempsey's Warehouse." An article from the *Miami Times-Herald* came up.

EXPLOSION LEVELS
WATERFRONT WAREHOUSE

Special to the Times-Herald:

An explosion of unknown origin occurred at the Dempsey's Warehouse on 14th Street. The explosion, which occurred just after midnight, killed three men who were working in the building at the time.

Although natural causes have not been ruled out, the warehouse has been cited in the past for being a known repository for drugs being shipped into the country. Because of that, police are working on the theory that the explosion was drug-related.

Don picked up the phone and tapped in the numbers.

"Yes?" John's voice said from the other end.

"I have something you might want to see," Don said.

By the time John arrived at the computer room, Don had already spread the printout on a table.

"What do you have?" John asked.

"This is the Chicago bomb, this is the St. Louis bomb," Don said, pointing to the printouts. "As you can see, the signatures are exactly the same."

John chuckled. "Not that I can see. I have no idea what I'm looking at here. But I'll take your word for it." He stared at the pages for a moment. "Any chance of this being a random match?" John asked.

"Practically none," Don answered. "Especially when you add this one." He put the third page down. This was the one about the warehouse explosion.

"Whoa," John said, picking it up. "What are you telling me? That we've got another one that matches?"

"Yes."

"Has there been a new bombing?"

"No, and that is what is interesting," Don said. "Here is a photograph of this blast." Don dropped an eight-by-ten picture of a blackened and destroyed building on the table. It took John only a couple of seconds to identify it.

"This was the warehouse in Miami, wasn't it?"

"Yes," Don answered. "And if memory serves me, we, that is, the Code Name Team, thought it might be the work of Pablo Bustamante."

"Pablo Bustamante, yes," John said. "One of the biggest drug lords in America. And you say the signatures of all three match?"

"Yes."

"Well, now, wait a minute. What connection does Bustamante have with Cesar Adib Jubair? He was a Muslim. Not an Arab, but a Muslim."

"I just make the connections," Don said. "I don't explain them."

* * *

Dallas, Texas

Amber left her BMW in the parking garage of the Galleria Shopping Center, took the gaily wrapped Christmas package from the front seat, then started into the mall. The Galleria was filled with Christmas shoppers, and holiday music played over the speaker system filling the shoppers with the proper spirit. The proper spirit, of course, at least as far as the mall association was concerned, was the spirit of buying. And if the number of package-carrying customers was any indication, the spirit was in full swing.

"Oh, what a lovely package you have, my dear," an elderly woman said as Amber passed her on the way into the mall. "That's going to give someone quite a surprise."

"Yes, it is," Amber replied.

At one key location in the Galleria a huge, beautifully decorated Christmas tree was drawing a large crowd of admirers. The tree, dominating the mall as it did, served as a meeting place for families separated by shopping missions to the various stores. Amber went to the tree, arming the bomb by pulling on a string that was concealed by the bright red bow. She put the package under the tree, then concealed it by moving one of the other packages that were already there. With the bomb armed, Amber had fifteen minutes to get away. Hurrying from the mall, she was already out on LBJ when the bomb went off. Of course, she was too far away from it to hear anything, but she turned on the radio to an all-news station. She didn't have long to wait.

"This just in. A bomb has exploded in the Galleria Mall in Dallas. Police and emergency workers are on the scene now, and though early details are still sketchy, sources on the scene have reported that casualties are heavy, with many known to be dead."

* * *

World News Network, New York

Lauren Day, host for the top-rated *American Afternoon* show, was going over the information she had on Harriet Clayton. Although Harriet was perhaps the most recognizable woman in America, and perhaps in the world, she had managed through her husband's long political career (in which she was a nearly equal partner) to keep her personal life in the background. There were vague rumors about her, about a fraudulent land-investment scheme back in South Amberina, shady billing practices in the Tulip Law Firm, where she had once been a junior partner, and even darker questions about her sexual preference.

It was Lauren's job to learn as much as she could about this woman who would be President, so she studied all the information she could gather.

Harriet had met her husband when they were both students at Harvard. Politically savvy, Harriet helped Eddie get elected to the State Senate, then as governor of South Carolina. While serving his second term as governor, Edward G. Clayton was tapped by the Presidential nominee, Jerome Jefferson, to run as his Vice President. The Jefferson-Clayton ticket won the election, but it was a tumultuous eight years, dominated by a special prosecutor's investigation of possible financial misdoings on the part of the President.

Clayton had his own scandal when a hooker sold her story about his late-night visits during which the Vice President would suck her toes. Despite that, Eddie Clayton managed to secure the nomination of his party for President, and though his loss was one of the narrowest in history, he did lose.

Some claimed that Harriet's campaign for the Senate, conducted at the same time as her husband's Presidential campaign, had actually undermined his efforts by preventing her from campaigning on his behalf. Others pointed out that Harriet's aggressive, acerbic personality was so controversial that Presidential candidate Edward Clayton was actually better off without his wife in the bitter campaign.

The phone rang on Lauren's desk.

"Yes?"

"Are you watching the news?" her producer asked.

"No, I'm prepping for the Harriet Clayton interview."

"Maybe you'd better give this a look," her producer said cryptically.

Picking up the remote on her desk, Lauren pointed it toward the TV that sat in the corner of her office. A beautiful mocha-skinned female news anchor was staring intently at the camera.

"We have a breaking story in Dallas, Texas," she said. "Several decorative ornaments on a large Christmas tree have burst, emitting some sort of gas. Authorities have stopped short of labeling it a terrorist attack, though they have not ruled that out. Details are sketchy at this time, but it is known that at least two have died in the incident."

Code Name Team Headquarters

"John, come back in here and watch this," Jennifer called.

"What is it?" John asked, coming back into the large living room.

"Something is happening in Dallas," Jennifer said.

First John, then the others came in to watch the story as it unfolded on the screen.

"You think it's terrorists?" Don asked.

"Yeah, I think it is. The question is, are we dealing with Muslim extremists here? Or is this more of Bustamante's work?"

As the members of the Code Name Team continued to watch the reports on the big-screen TV, Wagner started making secure telephone calls to get the latest inside reports from his contacts in the Department of Homeland Security. As a result, within one hour, the Code Name Team was better briefed than anyone else in the country.

They learned that twenty-two had died, nineteen from the effects of the bomb, while three had been trampled to death in the stampede trying to escape. In addition, 147 had been admitted to hospitals with a range of injuries from minor to critical.

The event was the lead story in all the TV and radio newscasts, and headline and front-page news in all newspapers. And as the day closed, the Department of Homeland Security elevated the warning level to orange.

World News Network, New York

"Going live in thirty," the floor director called. Three cameras moved into position as the AD adjusted Harriet Clayton's lavaliere microphone. Her fingers left a small dark smudge on Harriet's pink blouse.

"For God's sake, don't you ever wash your hands?" Harriet said irritably. She turned to Lauren. "Go to commercial or something," she ordered. "I can't go on with this stain on my blouse."

"It's not showing up on the preview monitor," someone said.

"Goddamnit, I said go to commercial!" Harriet snapped.

"Do it, Charley," Lauren said.

"All right, you've got two more minutes," the floor director replied.

The young assistant director hurried toward Harriet with a bottle of stain-remover.

"Not you," Harriet said. "You're the one that fouled my blouse in the first place. You'll just make it worse."

"I'm sorry, I just wanted to make amends," the AD said, holding up the bottle.

"If you really want to make amends, you'll go sit in a room somewhere until I'm gone," Harriet said.

"But . . ."

"It's all right, Pam, I'll take care of it," the floor director said. "Take a break."

"Yes, sir," Pam said. Tears streamed down her face as she hurried out of the studio.

"Where is the stain?" the floor director asked when he reached Harriet.

"What do you mean where is it? Are you blind as well as stupid?" Harriet asked irritably. She pointed to a tiny black dot just below her collar.

The floor director dabbed a small amount of stain-remover on the spot, and the tiny black dot went away. Within seconds, even the dampness of the cleaner had dried.

"Live in ten!" someone shouted, and the director moved quickly out of the picture. Harriet turned toward Lauren and put on a big smile, preparatory to facing the nation.

Lauren felt a sense of revulsion, and wished the entire country could have witnessed the episode that had just happened. She glanced toward Charley, and he was holding his fingers up, five-four-three-two-one.

The red light came on on the camera.

"Good afternoon," Lauren said with a professional smile pasted on her face. "I'm Lauren Day and you are watching *American Afternoon*. My guest today is Senator Harriet Clayton. Senator Clayton, thank you for coming on the show."

"Thank you very much for having me, Lauren," Harriet replied graciously.

"You are not only a Senator, you are also running for President. If you were the President of the United States, right now, what would you do with regard to the recent terrorist attack that took place in Dallas?"

"Well, Lauren, as I'm sure all Americans know, I was recently a hostage of Middle-Eastern terrorists and I got to know those people quite well. In fact, I am the only person running for President who has come face-to-face with them, and I understand their needs and desires. More than that, I know what motivates them. They want only the right to practice their religion without the interference of imperialistic America. And until we learn that we cannot, and should not, police the world, we are going to have to deal with events such as the one that just happened in Dallas."

"Then you believe the incident in Dallas was perpetrated by Muslim extremists?"

"I didn't say that," Harriet responded quickly. "What I said was that as long as we continue our military aggrandizing around the world, we are going to have to deal with incidents *like* what happened in Dallas."

"What about the bombings in Chicago and St. Louis? We now know that those were committed by the same person. And of course, he died in the St. Louis bombing."

"Yes, and I believe Jubair was Muslim," Harriet replied. She held up her finger. "Though I hasten to point out that he was Filipino, not Iraqi, Saudi, Iranian, or Sitarkistanian."

"Do you think there is any significance in the fact that he was Filipino?"

"Yes, a great deal of significance. It proves that our terrorist containment policy is not only failing, it is creating new terrorists outside the Middle East."

"And the recent sniper attacks in Mobile?"

"Obviously that has no connection at all," Harriet replied. "It was just random, senseless shootings, rather like the D.C. sniper shootings a few years ago."

"So, you see no connection between the sniper and the bomber?" Lauren Day asked.

"There are some who are saying that the bomber, Jubair, may be acting, not as a Muslim extremist, but out of personal revenge since the Army in the Philippines attacked his home village last year, killing one of his cousins."

"That was the Filipino Army, not our Army," Lauren replied.

"It makes no difference. It is well known that we have advisors in the Philippines, teaching their Army how to conduct terror raids against innocent civilians who want nothing more than the freedom to practice their own religion. That is another example of the cowboy attitude of our current administration to commit troops as a first option."

"Are you opposed to any type of military action?"

"Yes, I am."

"Under any circumstances? I mean, as you pointed out, you were once held hostage by these people What do you think would have happened to you if our government had not taken some military action to rescue you?"

"I would have been able to negotiate my own release," Harriet insisted.

"Do you seriously believe you could have negotiated with these people?"

"Yes," Harriet said. She looked into the camera, and the camera moved in for a close one-shot.

"This cycle of violence must stop," Harriet said. "If we do not get it stopped, then the killing will go on and on and nothing can protect us. Does our President really think that a three-billion-dollar airplane with a smart bomb could've prevented what happened at the Galleria Shopping Mall in Dallas? What would he have us do? Destroy the Galleria in order to save the Galleria?"

"But surely you would approve of some response," Lauren said.

Harriet shook her head. "Not if you are talking about military response," she replied.

"But if we do nothing, isn't that a sign of weakness? Wouldn't we just be opening ourselves for more attacks?"

"No," Harriet insisted. "By negotiating, we would be showing our strength . . . the strength of a nation that is so secure in its military power that we can forswear violence."

"There are some who believe that the attacks of nine-eleven were in fact brought about because the terrorists were emboldened by what happened in Somalia," Lauren suggested.

"What do you mean?"

"Well, there are those who say that, because we withdrew our troops after the incident there, that terrorists came to the belief that Americans had lost their will to fight. And as long as we give them reason to doubt our will, they will continue their attacks against us."

"Those arguments are made by the people who are quite willing to trade blood for oil," Harriet replied. "So long as it's not their blood that's being traded."

Lauren looked at the camera. "My guest today is United States Senator, and presidential candidate, Harriet Clayton. Stay tuned, we'll be back after these messages."

Fourteen

Zabakabad, Sitarkistan

Two men sat at a table in a sidewalk café on Avenue of the Heroes in Zabakabad. One of the men was dressed in traditional Arab dress, while the other wore Western clothing. As a waiter approached their table, the one in Arab clothing held up his finger as a signal to the waiter not to approach.

Pablo Bustamante poured whiskey from a small bottle into his coffee.

"As you can see, my friend, I have been able to deliver on my promise," Bustamante said. "Now it is time for you to hold up your end of the bargain."

"I had hoped that your effort would produce a more satisfying result," Jahmshidi said. "So far your efforts in Mobile, Chicago, St. Louis, and Dallas have killed relatively few. I am told that chain collisions on the highways often produce more fatalities."

Dallas had been a surprise to Pablo. It was nothing he had authorized; in fact, he didn't even know about it until he saw the story on the international broadcast of the World News Network. But if Jahmshidi wanted to credit him with it, he would take it.

"Here is a figure you might be interested in," Bustamante said. "As a result of the incidents in Chicago, St.

Louis, and Dallas, business analysts are predicting that Christmas shopping will be off by thirty percent this year."

"Is that significant?" Jahmshidi asked.

"Are you kidding? Most merchants count on Christmas shopping to supply up to one-third of their yearly receipts. This will have a crippling effect on the U.S. economy."

"What a blasphemous nation, to have so much of their economy dependent upon buying trinkets to celebrate the birth of their prophet," Jahmshidi said.

"Maybe so," Bustamante said. "But it is a fact of life and, right now, that fact is playing into our hands."

"You can do more?"

"Yes, I can do more. And I will do more," Bustamante said. "But so far, it's all been me. What are you doing to hold up your end of this bargain?"

"Even as we speak," Jahmshidi said, "a ship is being loaded with the raw material you need to make your devil's drug."

Bustamante smiled. "Some call it the devil's drug. Others say it is the key to paradise."

Jahmshidi looked up quickly, his dark eyes flashing in anger.

"There is only one key to paradise," he snapped. "And that is through Allah."

"Yes, I've seen some of those keys to paradise," Bustamante said. "I'm sure that every hijacker who crashed on September eleventh did so with a smile on his lips, certain that he was going straight to heaven."

"You demean those brave warriors of Allah while you yourself are committing acts of terror against your own country. I don't understand."

"Yes, well, I know that my few acts of terror aren't going to bring America down. Nor would I want it to. My business depends on Americans having the money to buy what I sell. Besides, I have a personal stake in the World Trade

Center. Maybe you don't know it, but I was at the World Trade Center on September tenth, just the day before your . . . martyrs . . . crashed into it. And I had planned to go back the next day, the day the planes crashed into the buildings, but something came up that kept me from going back."

"Allah."

"Allah? Allah what?"

"You said something came up that prevented you from returning to the World Trade Center. Allah is what came up. It is clear that Allah was not ready for you to die."

"Yeah? Well, now why would Allah want to protect a non-believer like me?"

"Because Allah had plans for you to serve him, as you are serving him now."

Bustamante laughed. "Yeah, well, listen, let's don't get the wrong idea about things here. You may look at what we are doing as serving Allah, but all I see is the profit to be made," he said.

"You are an infidel. Infidels will never be given the light to see the true faith," Jahmshidi said.

Bustamante chuckled. "Hell, no," he said. "Not as long as you keep killing them. Us," he amended.

"It is interesting that, for profit, you will kill your own kind."

"My own kind?"

"Infidels," Jahmshidi said.

"Yes, well, I understand there were some Muslims who were killed in the attack on nine-eleven. Is that true?"

"Yes," Jahmshidi said. "This is true."

"Well, don't you feel bad about them getting killed along with all the infidels?"

"No, I do not feel sorry for them," Jahmshidi said. "For if they were true believers, Allah will welcome them, and we did them a favor by sending them to paradise. If they were not true believers, then they went straight to hell and I have no sympathy for them."

"You are a cold man, Jahmshidi, to feel that way about your own kind."

"And you are a man without principles," Jahmshidi replied. "I do not expect a man such as yourself, a man without principles, to understand."

"Hah," Bustamante said. "You accuse me of being a man without principles, yet you are dealing in drugs. You are supplying me with what I need, even though you believe that is wrong. So I ask you, who is the greater sinner?"

"I can deal with my sin," Jahmshidi insisted. "For my sin is for the greater glory of Allah."

"Speaking of the greater glory of Allah, I understand you are enjoying the women I've been providing."

"I do not wish to discuss it," Jahmshidi said.

Bustamante laughed out loud. "I'm glad to see that there is one thing that is just alike among Muslims and Christians," he said.

"What is that?"

"Hypocrisy."

Code Name Team Headquarters

Don Yee was eating a bowl of chili as he and John Barrone studied black-and-white videotapes taken by the surveillance cameras of the Galleria in Dallas. Wagner had requested the tapes from a contact in Homeland Security and, under an outsourcing program, Homeland Security was authorized to make them available.

"Hold it, hold it!" John suddenly said. "Stop the tape."

"What is it? What do you see?"

"That woman. Don't you recognize her?"

Don looked at her for a moment. "Yeah," he said.

"Yeah, I do recognize her. I can't recall her name right now, but I know who she is."

"That's Amber D'Amour," John said.

"Yeah, I thought I recognized her. She's Bustamante's girlfriend, isn't she?"

"Girlfriend, one-time porn star, and from what we've heard, now full-time drug addict."

"I thought she was in Arizona. What's she doing in Dallas?"

"I have a better question. What is she doing carrying a Christmas-wrapped box into the mall?"

"It's Christmas."

"Think about it, Don. She's going *into* the mall with a box that is already Christmas-wrapped. Do you see anyone else going into the mall with a box that is already Christmas-wrapped?"

"Maybe she is taking it back."

"Huh-uh. If she was taking something back, she would have it in a sack, with a receipt. It wouldn't be Christmas-wrapped. What entrance is this, and what time was it taken?"

"This is the Macy's entrance off the parking garage," Don said. "It's 1133."

"The bomb went off when?"

"At 1155."

"Okay, let's look at the tree tapes again."

"We've looked at them a dozen times," Don said. "We've got a problem with the tape, remember? It was changed at about that time, so there is a ten-minute gap between 1135 and 1145."

"Yeah, but we didn't know what we were looking for then." John pointed toward the box Amber was carrying. "I want to see if that is under the tree."

"Oh, yeah, good idea," Don agreed. "It would be nice

if this was in color, though, wouldn't it? It would be easier to tell if she left the package there."

Don ran the tree tape through again.

"I don't see it, do you?" John asked.

"No, and I've counted the packages. The number of packages at 1135 is the same as it is at the time of the explosion," Don said.

"Yeah, I . . . wait a minute. Can you bring up stills from 1135, which is right after she arrived, and 1154, just before the explosion?"

"Sure," Don said, complying with John's request.

John studied the pictures for a moment; then he laughed.

"What is it?"

"You ever play that game on the comic pages in the paper? You know, where there are two pictures and you are supposed to look at them and tell what is different between them?"

"Yes," Don answered.

"Look at these two pictures. Look at the packages that are just to the right of the tree. Look at them at 1135, and again at 1154."

"I'll be damned! They've been moved."

"Yep. We didn't see the bomb being planted, because she did it during the ten minutes that the surveillance camera was off. And we didn't see the package, because she hid it behind some of the packages that were already there."

"I think you're right."

"Let's start looking at the entrances again," John said. "We need to find her leaving."

"That's a lot of tape."

"Not necessarily. Figure five minutes for her to get to the tree, and five minutes for her to get back, so we only have to check from about 1140 to 1150. You know she's going to be gone before the bomb goes off."

They had only been looking at the tapes for about ten minutes when Don called out, "Tally ho, the fucking fox!"

"You've found her?"

"She's leaving at 1143, the Nordstrom exit," Don said.

"What about the box?"

"She doesn't have it," Don said.

John turned his video player off, then leaned back in his chair and pinched the bridge of his nose.

"Forget people like Bin Laden, Khadaffi, and Jahmshidi," John said. "We've got our own home-grown terrorist, and his name is Pablo Bustamante."

"Yes," Don said. "I agree. But why?"

"We know the who," John said. "We'll figure out the why later. The most important thing now is what, where, and when the next one will be."

Fifteen

It was two A.M., and from the steady and rhythmic breathing she could hear coming from the other rooms in the house, Ly Kwan was certain that everyone else was asleep. As she had been doing for one hour every night for the previous two months, she took the cap off the top of her bedstead, then reached down to grasp a piece of thread.

A bent nail, tied to the other end of the thread, hung down into the hollow frame of the bed. Using the thread, Ly pulled the nail up, then with nail in hand, walked over to the door, knelt on the floor, and began to work.

Over the last several nights, Ly had used the nail to drill a series of small holes in the lower panel of the door. As each hole was finished, she would cover up the work by filling the hole with dirt so that no casual examination would disclose her handiwork.

It had been nearly one month since Ly arrived in Sitarkistan. She had resisted the sexual demands for the first few times, but beatings and starvation had left her no choice. So Ly had changed her strategy. Instead of resisting her captors, she cooperated with them, buying time to put her escape plan into operation.

Suddenly, and unexpectedly, the panel came loose in her hands. She was through!

Cautiously, Ly stuck her head out through the opening and looked around. Seeing no one there, she crawled through the opening, sneaked down the stairs, and quietly let herself out.

American embassy, Zabakabad, Sitarkistan

Ly Kwan had been at the American embassy for three days, waiting to hear what disposition was to be made of her. She had told them she was married to an American named Bill Smith, even though the two men who had brought her to Sitarkistan had told her the marriage was a fake.

She didn't believe it was a fake. Bill Smith had been too nice to her. She was certain that he really was her husband, and the two men who had brought her here had told her otherwise only as a means of controlling her.

Someone knocked on her door, and hoping that it might be news of her husband, she opened it eagerly.

"Yes?" she said. "You have news for me? You have found my husband?"

The embassy employee, Miss Margrabe, shook her head slowly. "I'm sorry," she said. "We can find no record of your marriage, or even your legal arrival in the States."

"But there must be some record somewhere," Ly insisted. "What about the people who brought me here?"

"I'm sorry. We found nothing on them either."

"Their names were Nelson and Brewer."

"Are those first names? Or last names?"

"I . . . I don't know."

"Without first and last names, any kind of a definitive search is impossible."

"What about my husband? His name is Bill Smith," Ly said.

"Yes, so you have said. Did you not try to contact him before you left the States?"

"I did not know how to call him."

"Miss Kwan, Bill Smith is a very common name, perhaps one of the most common names in America. There are hundreds of thousands of Bill Smiths. Is it possible that Bill Smith wasn't his real name?"

Ly thought of the conversation she'd had with Nelson and Brewer shortly before they left. "Perhaps it is possible," she admitted.

"And is it also possible that you weren't really married?"

"I thought I was married, but the men who took me said that I was not. I did not believe them. I do not believe them. I think if my husband knew where I was, he would come for me."

"Miss Kwan, you say you were brought here against your will and forced into prostitution against your will. Is that right?"

"Yes."

"And you've had no opportunity to contact the man you believe to be your husband since your kidnapping?"

"No."

"If the marriage had been authentic, don't you think there would have been a missing-persons report filed on you by now?"

"Missing-persons report?"

"Yes. Surely, once your husband discovered you were gone, he would have filed a missing-persons report. Unless . . ." Miss Margrabe let the word hang.

"Unless?"

"Unless he was a party to it all along. How well did you know him?"

"We were married," Ly Kwan insisted.

"Yes, you told me that. But how well did you know him? How long had you known him before you were married?"

"Only for a few days," Ly Kwan said. "The marriage was arranged."

"Arranged?"

"Yes. I answered an advertisement that said American men were looking for Chinese wives."

"And you came all the way to America to marry a man you had never met before?"

"Arranged marriages are very common in China," Ly said defensively. "They are an honorable way to begin a family."

"Yes, well, they aren't quite that common in the States. I hate to tell you this, Miss Kwan, but I'm convinced that the man you think is your husband is part of a white-slavery operation."

"White slavery, yes," Ly said, recalling the explanation Brenda had given her.

"White slavery is quite common here in the Middle East. And I'm afraid that is what has happened to you."

"I don't know about such things," Ly said. "I know only that I want to go back to America."

"That isn't possible," Miss Margrabe said.

"Then. . . what will happen to me now?" Ly asked.

"You say you have family in China?"

"Yes."

"We can take you to the Chinese embassy," Miss Margrabe said. "I'm sure they can help you."

"Thank you," Ly said. "I believe now that I would like to go home."

* * *

Chinese embassy

"Our records show that you left China for America," the clerk at the Chinese embassy said.

"Yes, this is true. I married an American."

"Then you are not our problem. You are the problem of the United States."

"I went to the American Embassy. They have no record of me marrying an American. They say I am Chinese. Please, I just want to go home."

"You have no home," the clerk said. "You gave up your home when you left for America."

"But where will I go?" Ly Kwan asked.

"That is none of our concern," the clerk replied. He glanced toward one of the uniformed guards. "Escort her out of the embassy," he ordered.

Addison, Texas

CIA Operative Tom Harold was contacted by the Code Name Team, and a meeting was set up in Addison, which is a suburb of Dallas. And as usual, when in Addison, they made reservations at the Texas de Brazil restaurant, located on the corner of Addison and Beltline. Texas de Brazil was a very good, if somewhat pricey, restaurant, and they chose it, not only for the food, but also because of its proximity to the Addison airport. Don had flown John and himself to Addison, where they were to meet with Tom Harold.

John and Don met Harold's flight at DFW, then drove him to the Texas de Brazil for lunch. Once they were seated, the waiter brought around skewers of barbecued meat, including lamb, beef, pork, and chicken.

"You have your choice of meat, gentlemen," the waiter said.

"Still no limit?" Don asked.

"Enjoy yourself, Mr. Yee. As soon as we learned you were coming, the manager put on two extra cooks to take care of you."

John and the others laughed.

"Good. I'll take the lamb."

The waiter started to slice off a sizeable portion of meat, then, remembering Don from previous visits, just put the entire skewer on his plate.

"And as usual, you will want beef, pork, and chicken?" the waiter asked.

"Yes, but maybe only half a skewer of each," Don said.

"Very good, sir," the waiter replied.

The subject of Tom Harold's visit wasn't brought up until all the plates were filled and the waiter had withdrawn.

"All right, John, so what's up?" Tom asked as they started their meal.

"I have something I would like you to see," John said. Reaching down into his briefcase, he pulled out a manila folder, opened it, and removed a picture. "Do you recognize her?"

Harold stared at the picture for a moment.

"No, I can't say as I do," he said.

"I apologize for it not being all that clear," John said. "It's a still taken from a security camera. But we believe this is the person who set off the bomb at the Galleria."

"The hell you say," Harold replied. He picked up the picture and studied it more closely. "What's her name?"

"D'Amour. Amber D'Amour," John replied.

"Amber D'Amour? Why is that name familiar?"

"Well, if you watch many porn movies, you might recognize it," Don teased.

Harold laughed. "I don't see that many of them."

"She's also Pablo Bustamante's girlfriend," John said.

"Ah-ha! Yeah, I knew I had heard the name," Harold said. "So, what are you telling me? That you think she is the one who planted the bomb?"

"Oh, I don't just think she did it, I know she did it."

"But why? In the first place, why would Bustamante be involved in terrorist activity? I mean, come on, I know he is a bad guy, but terrorism? That just doesn't fit his profile."

"Perhaps not," John replied. "But we think we can connect him to all the other recent events as well. The bombings in Chicago and St. Louis . . ."

"Wait a minute, that was Cesar Adib Jubair, a known Muslim extremist," Harold said. "What does he have to do with Bustamante?"

"We don't know yet. We only know that there is a connection, and not only with the bombings, but with the sniper in Mobile."

"We have now matched the Chicago, St. Louis, and Dallas bomb with the one that destroyed the Dempsey Warehouse in Miami a few years ago," Don said.

"The Dempsey Warehouse?" Harold asked.

"I know the CIA isn't up to speed on this, but DEA suspects that was a Bustamante operation," John explained. "That connection, with Amber D'Amour, ties them all together for me."

"And don't forget the money," Don said.

"What money?" Harold asked.

John told about the deposits that were made before each incident.

"Including the sniper killings in Mobile," Don added.

"At this point it is all circumstantial, but it sure looks like Bustamante is right in the middle of this. The question is, why?"

"Maybe this is why," Tom Harold said, taking out a CD. "You didn't get this from me."

Back at Code Name Headquarters, Don began working on the CD that Harold had provided. As he knew it would, the CD was encoded. But because they had worked with the CIA several times in the past, Don had access to the code, and he applied it now to open up the document. As soon as he had it in the clear, he picked up the phone and called John.

"I've got it," he said.

"I'll be right there."

TOP SECRET
FOR EYES ONLY

In-country assets in Sitarkistan report several meetings between Jahmshidi Mehdi and Pablo Bustamante. Though we have been unable to ascertain the purpose of the meetings, it is believed that Jahmshidi might be supplying drugs to Bustamante, in exchange for money he uses in his terrorist activities.

"Damn," John said. "I know what it is. I know the connection now."

"What?" Jennifer asked.

"The incident at the bank in New Orleans took away his ability to pay cash for his drugs. He's bartering for them."

"What do you mean, bartering?" Chris asked.

"He's committing acts of terror in exchange for drugs."

* * *

American embassy, Zabakabad, Sitarkistan

One of Prunella Margrabe's regular jobs was to read the newspapers. Since Sitarkistan had been a British possession for many years, English was one of the two official languages and the principal newspapers were published in that language.

As Miss Margrabe perused the front page, she suddenly gasped, then put her hand to her mouth.

"Oh!" she said. "Oh, dear, that poor girl."

"What is it, Pru?" one of the other embassy employees asked. "What are you talking about?"

"Paul, you remember the young Chinese girl who stayed with us for a while?"

"Yeah, sure I do. She was a good-looking woman. Hard to forget her. What about her?"

"She's dead," Miss Margrabe said.

"Dead? How?"

"Evidently, she was the victim of a mugging," Miss Margrabe said. "The police don't even know her name."

"There's no name? Then how do you know it's the same one?" Paul asked.

"You look at it," she suggested, handing over the newspaper and pointing to the picture.

The picture was of a young Chinese woman who had obviously been badly beaten.

Paul glanced at it only briefly, then shook his head.

"Oh, yes, it is her all right," Miss Margrabe insisted. "Look more closely."

When Paul took a second look, his disbelief changed to reluctant acceptance. Sighing, he nodded his head. "Yes," he said. "I'm afraid you are right."

Miss Margrabe picked up the phone.

"What are you doing?"

"The police have asked for assistance in identifying her," Miss Margrabe said.

It had been Miss Margrabe's intention merely to call and identify Ly Kwan over the phone, but the police asked her to come down to the station to view the body. It wasn't something she wanted to do, but she felt that she had no choice.

"We believe she was a pleasure-harem girl," Chief Ashar Hakid said as he led Miss Margrabe toward the morgue.

"A pleasure-harem girl?"

"Yes, young women who enter into a contract with a procurer in order to sell sexual favors." He pulled open a drawer and Miss Margrabe looked down at the body. The face was disfigured, not only by the beating that killed her, but also by the fact that she had been dead for a few days. "Do you know her?" he asked.

Miss Margrabe put a handkerchief to her face and turned away. "Yes," she said. "It is Ly Kwan."

"Thank you." Hakid closed the drawer.

"But she didn't sell herself into prostitution," Miss Margrabe said. "She was brought here against her will, and she was held prisoner."

Hakid laughed. "Yes, yes, I've such stories before. They are myths, you know."

"Myths?"

"The idea that there are such operations going on in our country. Not only our country, nearly every country in the Middle East has been accused of participating in white slavery."

"White slavery, yes."

"Well, as I said, it is a myth."

"She was adamant about the fact that she had been brought here against her will," Miss Margrabe insisted.

"Oh, I'm sure that's the story she told you. But the truth is, she probably became dissatisfied with her contract and wanted some way to get out of it. Believe me, I have personally investigated these allegations time after time, and I've never found the slightest bit of evidence to substantiate the claim."

"She wanted to get out of her contract? What do you mean by contract?"

"Sitarkistan women are prohibited from engaging in prostitution," Hakid explained. "In fact, the penalty for prostitution, and for adultery, is death."

"Yes, I've read about some of your executions," Miss Margrabe replied.

"But we are an enlightened country in that we recognize that our men need some outlet for their sexual stress. Therefore our law allows contracted concubines. Of course, that is for foreign women only. We would never think of subjecting Sitarkistan women to such indignity."

"No, I'm sure you wouldn't," Miss Margrabe said dryly, though her sarcasm was lost on Hakid.

"I believe you will find that your Miss Ly Kwan was just such a woman. She was here under contract to perform sexual services."

"If so, she wanted out."

"That may be, but a contract is a contract after all."

"What do you think happened to her?"

"I'm sure she got into some disagreement over the amount of money she was charging for her services. The disagreement became violent, and she was killed. I don't think the person who did this meant to kill her."

"Are you serious? Did you see how badly beaten she was?"

"Yes, and that's what makes me think that whoever did this had no intention of killing her. I think he was just very angry, probably justifiably so, and . . ."

"Justifiably?" Miss Margrabe asked, her voice rising sharply.

"Well, justifiable only in a manner of speaking," Hakid said. "She probably quoted him one price, then changed it. It has happened before."

"You are going to hunt for her killer, aren't you?"

"We will ask around to determine if anyone saw a young Chinese woman and, if so, who she was with. But these things nearly always happen in back rooms somewhere. I'm certain there are no witnesses, which means we probably won't come up with anything."

"No. You probably won't," Miss Margrabe replied, the expression in her voice showing her disdain for the police chief.

Sixteen

Fountain Hills, Arizona

Baldwin Carter was surprised to see Amber when she drove up in the driveway. Seeing the look on his face, Amber giggled as she got out of the car.

"Hello, Baldwin," she called gaily. "I'll bet you didn't expect to see me again, did you?"

"No, I didn't," Baldwin replied.

"I thought you might be surprised. I like surprises. I've got one for Pablo. Is he here?"

"No, he hasn't returned."

"Well, that's all right. I'll just make myself at home until he does return. You haven't cleaned out my room yet, have you?"

"No, your room is just as you left it."

"When will Pablo be back?"

"Not for several days," Baldwin said.

"That's okay. I'll wait."

Guardian Angel Island

Mendoza showed Bustamante around while the shipment of raw material was unloaded. The warehouses and processing sheds were all up and running.

"You've done well," Bustamante said. "What about security?"

"An army couldn't get in here," Mendoza promised. "We have twenty armed guards, concertina wire and claymore mines on the beaches, and towers that allow observation of the entire island."

"You're convinced you can keep me supplied?"

"Thirty days from now you'll have more product on the street from your own factory than you ever got from your contacts in Colombia."

"Good. I'm counting on that."

"All I ask is that you keep the raw material coming."

"Don't you worry about that," Bustamante said. "I've got it well in hand."

Baldwin met Bustamante in the driveway when he returned. Bustamante stretched tiredly as the house servants started unloading his luggage.

"Good trip?" Baldwin asked.

"Good, yes. But tiring. I came back on the ship. Remind me not to take any more ocean cruises. I was seasick half . . ." Bustamante stopped in mid-sentence, then pointed to Amber's BMW. "Is that Amber's car?"

"Yes."

"What the hell is that bitch doing here? I told her I wanted her ass gone when I got back."

"She says she has a surprise for you," Baldwin said.

"A surprise? What kind of surprise?"

"I don't know, she didn't share that. She just said that she had a surprise that would change your mind, make you want her to stay."

"There is absolutely nothing that bitch could do that would make me want her to stay," Bustamante said, starting toward the house. "Where is she? In her room?"

"I believe so."

"Pablo! Welcome home!" Amber greeted him effusively when Bustamante stormed, without knocking, into her room.

"What the hell are you doing here?" Bustamante asked gruffly. "I told you I wanted you out of here when I came back."

"You'll change your mind once I tell you my surprise," Amber said.

"Surprise? What surprise? Son of a bitch! You aren't pregnant, are you?"

For a second, Amber looked shocked. Then she laughed. "Pregnant? Me? Oh, sweetheart, don't you think I've learned by now how to keep from getting pregnant? No, my surprise for you is Dallas."

"Dallas?"

"Didn't you see any news at all while you were gone?" Amber asked. "Didn't you hear about Dallas? It made the covers of all the news magazines. They are calling it the Christmas Bombing."

Bustamante's eyes narrowed. "You did that?"

"Yes," Amber said proudly.

"Why?"

"Why, for you, or course."

"Well, I'll be damned."

"Are you pleased?"

"Yes."

"So, does that mean I can stay?"

"Yes," Bustamante said. "You can stay."

* * *

Bustamante had been home for two days and was still recovering from the travel. He was in his den watching a porn film when Baldwin Carter came into the room. Baldwin cleared his throat to get Bustamante's attention.

"You sure chose a hell of a time to interrupt me, Baldwin. Can't you see that these two women are about to go down on each other?"

"Yes, sir. It's about Miss D'Amour."

"Yeah? What about her?"

"I'm afraid she's dead, sir."

Bustamante showed little reaction to the news as he glanced up from the movie. "Dead?"

"Yes, sir. I'm afraid so."

"OD'd?"

"Apparently so," Baldwin answered. "One of the servants found her lying in a lounge chair out on the patio."

"I see."

"So, what do we do now? Who do we call? The police? The funeral home?" Baldwin asked.

"Hell, no, don't call the police," Bustamante said. "The last thing I want is for the police to be poking around out here." Bustamante stroked his chin for a moment while thinking about his next move. "Is the gardener here?"

"Yes, sir, I believe he is."

"Send him in to me."

As Baldwin left to summon the gardener, Bustamante thought about Amber. In fact, he had been thinking about her a great deal lately, because she was beginning to become a problem. Her drug habit made her very unreliable, and he couldn't afford to be surrounded by unreliable people, especially someone who knew as much about his business as Amber did. It was just pure luck that she wasn't caught doing the Dallas job. If she had been caught, she would have led them right back to him.

Now the problem was resolved. Amber had taken care of it herself when she overdosed. Of course, he might have helped just a little when he replaced her stash with a supply that was ten times more potent than anything she was used to.

Smiling, Bustamante picked up the remote and pointed it at the DVD. He ran it back to the point where the two women had begun undressing each other.

"Now," he said under his breath. "Let's see what you girls can do."

It was dark, more so because the night was moonless, and the wind whistled through the saguaro cactus and made the overhead power transmission lines sing. Mesquite limbs bent in the wind, and a lizard looked up as an old pickup truck approached.

The truck stopped and the engine was killed, but the headlights remained on, their twin beams stabbing into the darkness ahead. The doors slammed shut and two men got out, then walked back to the bed of the truck and looked down at the tarpaulin.

"Ramon, get the shovels," the driver said.

"I don't like this, Pedro," Ramon said. "I don't like this at all."

"Are you crazy? We are getting ten thousand dollars apiece just to dig a hole in the ground."

"No. We are getting ten thousand dollars apiece to bury a woman's body," Ramon said. "What if someone came along now and saw us?"

"It's four o'clock in the morning. Who is going to be out at four in the morning?"

"Still, we could get in a lot of trouble."

"How? We did not do anything," Pedro said. "I saw her come out to the pool. Then she died."

"She should have a real burial, I think."

"What do you mean a real burial?"

"She should be buried by a priest, who should say some words over her. I do not believe she should be buried like a dead dog."

"No church would let this woman be buried in their cemetery, and no priest would say words over her. Anyway, she is dead," Pedro said. "So what difference does it make? She will not know what kind of burial she has. And she has no family, so no one else will know."

"I will know."

"If you want to say some prayers for her, go ahead. But get the shovels."

Ramon got the spades, handed one of them to Pedro, and the two men started digging a hole in the desert floor. The wind began to blow even harder, and the singing through the wires sounded like moans.

"Listen," Ramon said. "The devil is calling to us."

Pedro laughed, then pulled a bottle of tequila from his back pocket. He took a couple of swallows, then handed the bottle to Ramon.

"Here," he said. "Drink some courage."

When the hole was finished, they returned to the truck, then removed the tarpaulin. Amber was lying there, still and cold, still wearing the bikini she had worn while out by the pool.

"She was a beautiful woman," Ramon said.

"Yes. The devil will be happy to see her. He will make her his mistress, I think," Pedro said with another laugh. He took another drink of tequila.

"Pedro, do not say such a thing," Ramon said. Looking at Amber's body, he crossed himself. "Let us do this evil thing quickly, and get out of here," he said.

The two men carried the body over to the hole, then dropped her in. She hit the bottom of the hole, then turned on her side. Ramon started to climb down into the hole.

"What are you doing?" Pedro asked.

"We can't bury her like this. She should be on her back, looking up toward heaven."

"Looking toward heaven? Believe me, Ramon, that is not where this one will go. So, if you are going to say words, now is the time to do it."

Again, Ramon crossed himself. "Lord," he started. He hesitated for a moment, then started again. "Lord." Again he paused for a long moment, then looked over at Ramon. "I can't think of anything to say," he said.

"Good. For this one, a good prayer would be a waste, I think." Pedro threw a shovel load of dirt down onto the body and, after a moment of hesitation, Ramon began throwing in the dirt as well.

"What are you going to do with your money, Ramon?" Pedro asked as the two men worked to cover the body.

"I don't know yet," Ramon replied. "What will you do?"

"I'm going to buy a better truck," Pedro said. "A red one."

Code Name Team Headquarters

The name of the website was International Connections, and it promised those who signed on a way of meeting others "for stimulating chat and interesting and profitable relationships." On the surface, it seemed like just another type of Internet dating service, but Don Yee, the Code Name Team's computer guru, discovered that it was much more sinister than that.

"This is the gateway to Bustamante's white slavery operation," he explained to the others from the team. "Young women sign onto the site, thinking this is a social and economic opportunity to meet someone new and exciting. In most cases, the women are foreigners, hoping for a quick way to permanent residency in America."

"A quick way to permanent residency?" Jennifer Barnes asked.

"Yes, by marrying an American citizen, they are granted an immediate permanent-residency status."

"I take it not many marriages occur?" Linda Marsh asked.

"Well, yes and no," Don replied.

Jennifer Barnes laughed. "You covered all the bases there, Don. Whether the answer is yes or no, you are right."

Don laughed as well.

"It's not a question you can answer directly," he said. "When the women arrive, there *is* a marriage, complete with a wedding ceremony. But the whole thing is a farce. The 'preacher' who marries them is as phony as the marriage license that is issued. Shortly afterward, their 'husband' sells them into a prostitution ring."

"Why don't the women go to the police to complain?"

"That would work if they were still in America. But for the most part, the prostitution ring is international and, more often than not, the women wind up in the Middle East. There, they are kept as virtual prisoners. They are truly slaves to their masters."

"Well, isn't slavery illegal over there?"

"Supposedly it is illegal. But it is such a profitable operation that the police turn a blind eye to it. Although most people don't realize it, the world has more slaves today than at any time in history."

"That's awful," Jennifer said.

"Yes," Linda agreed. "Someone should do something about it."

"I was hoping you would say that, Linda," John said. "Because if we undertake this operation, you are the perfect person for the job."

"Uh-oh," Linda said. "I knew I should've kept my mouth shut."

"It is purely voluntary on your part," John said. "But this may well be the best way to get someone inside Bustamante's operation."

"Let me get this straight. You want Linda to become one of these white slaves?" Jennifer asked.

"Yes, that's what I had in mind," John replied.

"How do you feel about this, Linda?" Jennifer asked.

"I don't have any feelings about it one way or the other," Linda said. "If this is what I'm expected to do, I'll do it." She smiled. "Besides, how hard can it be to act like a slut? Hell, folks been accusing me of that ever since I was twelve years old."

"Lest you take this too lightly, perhaps you should look at this," Don suggested. He showed Linda and the others a newspaper article.

"This didn't make the front page of any paper in Sitarkistan," Don said. "I don't know if it is because they are embarrassed by it . . . or that the incident just didn't seem important enough to them."

At the top of the article was a picture of a young Chinese woman. She might have been attractive at one time, but her face showed the strains of the life she had been living and the marks of the beating she had died from.

"This is how I discovered Bustamante's gateway," Don said. "This is . . . or was . . . Ly Kwan." He was silent for a moment. "She was my cousin."

"Oh, Don, I'm so sorry," Jennifer said.

"From what I've been able to find out, Ly showed up at the American embassy in Zibakabad, Sitarkistan, claiming to be married to an American. She said she had been captured in the U.S., then taken against her will to

Sitarkistan, where she was held as a slave. She escaped, then went to our embassy, where she asked for help."

"And we didn't help her?"

"When our embassy checked her story, they found no record of her marriage, so they could do nothing for her."

"So our embassy did what? Sent her back to her slave master?" Linda asked. "I thought the Fugitive Slave Act had been repealed."

"No. Our embassy sent her to the Chinese, but they didn't want anything to do with her either, so she was turned over to the Zibakabad Police. Two days later her body was found in the Nyambui River."

"That's rough," Linda said.

"Are you still willing to do this?" John asked.

Linda was silent for a moment, then nodded affirmatively. "Yes, I'll do it," she said.

"Good girl," John said. He stared at her for a second, then laughed.

"What is it?"

"You're going to make some sultan a beautiful addition to his harem," John said.

With her dark, flashing eyes, coal-black hair, and olive complexion, Linda was one of those beauties whose ethnic makeup could not be easily ascertained. There was a reason for that. Linda's genetic background was as exotic as her looks.

"When do we start?"

"Whoa, Linda, wait a minute," Jennifer said. "You might want to think about this for a moment. This isn't going to be a walk in the park."

Linda laughed. "Now, just when is the last time you, or I, or any of us did something that was a walk in the park?" she asked.

"I know, but this is different."

"How different?"

"Just . . . different," Jennifer replied, without offering any more explanation.

"Jennifer, look at me," Linda said. "What do you see?"

"What do you mean, what do I see? I see a beautiful, brave, and talented woman who is also my friend."

"Maybe so, but I'm not what you would call a WASP, am I?"

"Okay, you aren't white Anglo-Saxon Protestant. So what?"

"I'm also not Hispanic, Oriental, African-American, or Mid-Eastern. When I was a schoolchild, we had to identify ourselves by race on our school-registration cards. I remember, vividly, my confusion, and my anger, when the teacher told me to check 'other.' I wouldn't do that, so I came up with another solution."

"What was that?"

"I drew an additional little box," Linda said. "I labeled it 'All' and checked it."

Jennifer and the others laughed.

"So you see, if they are specializing in non-WASP-type women, then I feel a visceral connection to this evil. And if the only way we can do something about it is for me to get inside . . . as a white slave, I'll do it." Inexplicably, she laughed.

"What is it? What is so funny?"

"Come to think of it," Linda said, "I wouldn't miss this opportunity for the world. It might be the only time I've ever been able to refer to myself, unequivocally, as 'white,' at least as far as the 'white slavery' part."

Again, the others laughed.

"All right, Don, how do we get her inside?" Mike asked.

Don punched a few keys on his computer, and an Internet page came up.

"American men looking for exotic beautiful, non-American women for matrimony" it read. "If you are such a person, and would be interested in marrying a kind, providing, and loving American man, please respond."

"What sort of exotic, beautiful, non-American woman would you like to be?" Don asked.

"My name is Pilar Valdez," Linda said. "I am Colombian."

Don typed in the information and, a moment later, an instant message appeared on the screen. The message was in Spanish.

"It's in Spanish," Don said. "I should've thought of that. This may be some sort of preliminary evaluation as to the authenticity of the response."

"No problem," Linda said. "I chose Colombia rather than Lebanon because my Spanish is better than my Arabic. They are asking how old I am. Tell them I am twenty-eight."

Don started to type, but Jennifer reached down to stop him.

"No, wait," she said. "Better make her younger than that. Make her nineteen."

"Nineteen?" Linda said. She laughed. "It would take a makeup genius to make me look nineteen."

Jennifer smiled. "Honey, I *am* a makeup genius," she said.

"But why nineteen? Isn't that a little young?"

"If I thought we could make it fly, I'd tell them you are fourteen," Jennifer said. "For the perverts who make up the clientele of these assholes, the younger you are, the better."

"She's right," John said. "The younger you are, the better."

"I don't know," Linda said. She put her hand to her face. "Nineteen? I could never pass for nineteen."

"Sure you can," Jennifer said. "After all, that's one of the things I hate about you beautiful exotic-looking bitches. Come with me. Through the magic of makeup, we are going to turn back the clock twenty years."

"What? Twenty years? Why, you!" Linda said, chasing a laughing Jennifer out of the room.

Seventeen

A huge picture of a smiling Harriet Clayton was on front of a three-story brick building located on the corner of Lafayette and Broad. The windows and the door of the building were draped with red, white, and blue bunting. A huge white banner, with words in black, HAR-RIET CLAYTON NATIONAL HEADQUARTERS, was stretched across the front, just under the eaves.

Inside, the building was a beehive of activity with ringing telephones, clacking computer keyboards, and running printers. A heavy-set, middle-aged black woman sat at her desk in front. As she checked the latest polling data on a computer printout sheet, others kept dropping by her desk, asking questions and receiving directions, indicative of LaTisha Waters's position as the person in charge. "Miss Waters," one of the young campaign workers called. "Miss Waters, this phone call is for you."

"Whoever it is, tell them I'll call them back," LaTisha said.

"It's Mr. Norton," the young campaign worker replied. "He and the Senator are on their way here."

LaTisha picked up the phone. "Hello, Henry," she said.

"Is the reporter from *National News Magazine* there?" Henry asked.

"Oh, yes. She's been here for almost an hour. Where are you? I thought you and the Senator would be here by now."

"We're on our way from the airport now. We were late getting off the ground in Cleveland," Henry said. "Don't let the reporter leave; we'll be there in half an hour."

"All right. Oh, our poll numbers are in from the early primary states and they are looking very good."

"Good, good," Henry said.

As LaTisha continued her conversation, the young woman who had called her to the phone now went out back with a wastebasket full of shredded paper. She emptied it into the Dempsey Dumpster and, looking down the alley, saw a rental truck at the far end. She watched it for a moment, but the truck did not appear to be coming any farther up the alley.

That was good, the young woman thought. She went back inside, glad that the truck wasn't coming here, because every time one did, the entire staff would have to unload it. And as there were many more women than men on the election headquarters staff, that meant the women had to be involved in all the lifting and carrying.

Dexter Pogue stopped the truck when he saw the young woman come out of the back of the building. He sat there until she went back inside, then drove the rest of the way down the alley, maneuvering the truck carefully around the Dempsey Dumpster the young woman had just used. He stopped it right behind the back door of the headquarters building, then killed the engine. Just before he got out of the truck, he flipped a small toggle switch and, immediately, a digital readout in red began counting down from 20:00 to 19:59, 19:58, and so on. Pogue stood outside the cab of the truck for a few seconds, just to make certain the timer was activated. Once he was satisfied that everything was working properly, he walked rather quickly back down to the end of the alley, then crossed the street and went into a coffee shop. There, he found a seat near the window that would afford him a view of the campaign headquarters building.

A waitress, popping the gum she was chewing, walked over to the table, then stood in a way that thrust one hip out as she pulled a pencil from her hair. "What can I get you, honey?" she asked. Her accent was flat and familiar.

"Now, what's a Southern girl like you doin' up here in Yankee land?" Pogue asked.

"Whooee, if it don't sound good to hear a voice from home," the woman said. "Where you from?"

"Alabama."

"Georgia myself," the waitress said. "I married a Yankee soldier and come up here with him when he got out of the Army. Only, me'n him is divorced now."

"How come you ain't gone back home?"

"Don't think I don't want to," the waitress replied. "But the divorce says I can't take my little boy out of the state unless I have his father's permission."

"Bummer," Pogue said. "I'll have a cup of coffee."

"Cream and sugar?"

"Don't need none," Pogue said. "Just stick your thumb in it, that'll be all the sweetenin' I'll need."

"Whooee, ain't you somethin', though?" the waitress said as she left to take care of his order.

Pogue looked around the little café. In addition to the waitress . . . her tag said her name was Mabel . . . there were three other customers. One man who was sitting at the counter, drinking coffee and reading a newspaper, and a couple sitting in a booth in the back, eating hamburgers and talking and laughing quietly across the table that separated them.

Pogue checked his watch and looked through the window. There were six minutes remaining.

Mabel brought the coffee to his table

"We got some pretty good apple pie," Mabel said. "We don't make it here in the café, but it's pretty good."

"Okay, bring me a piece."

Pogue looked at his watch. Just under three minutes now. He stared through the window at the front of the campaign headquarters building, half a block down and on the other side of Lafayette.

Mabel returned with the pie. "I get off at seven," she said.

"What?"

"I get off at seven," she repeated.

Pogue smiled. "I'll remember that," he said.

It was nearly rush hour, and traffic was getting heavier on the street. Pogue checked his watch again, and drummed his fingers nervously as he waited.

He didn't know why he was nervous now. If he was going to be nervous, he should've been nervous yesterday morning when he picked up the truck in Atlanta. The back end of the truck was filled with ammonium nitrate, as much explosive as Timothy McVeigh had had for the Murrah Federal Building. It had been nerve-racking coming up I-95, knowing that the slightest fender-bender could turn him into dust.

Back inside the campaign headquarters, the work continued. Word had already spread through the building that Senator Clayton would be there within half an hour and the workers, many of them volunteers, were growing excited over the prospect of being in such close proximity to the woman who had become a superstar in her party.

LaTisha finished reviewing the poll number printouts, and leaned over to put the papers in her holding basket. At that moment she just happened to glance up toward the large picture of Harriet that was on the back wall. As she did so, she was amazed to see that the picture seemed to be moving toward her. Even as she was wondering how this was possible, the wall broke up, turning into several large black chunks of material, surrounded by a flash of white-hot light.

The rupturing wall allowed the shock wave of the explosion to rush through the building. That had the effect of turning cinder blocks, bricks, desks, computers, and filing cabinets into massive pieces of shrapnel. LaTisha didn't see all that, however, for a large chunk of debris struck her in the head, killing her instantly.

Pogue was looking right at the campaign headquarters when he saw a brilliant flash of light, followed almost immediately by debris and smoke and, a few seconds later, the rumbling thump of the explosion. The explosion was so loud that the windows of the café rattled, as did the glasses and china on the tables.

"My Lord in heaven, what was that?" Mabel shouted.

"Oh, my God!" the man at the end of the counter yelled said. "One of the buildings down the street just exploded!"

"It's terrorists! They've hit Newark!" a man shouted, running into the café at that time. The woman in the booth in back screamed.

The blast not only leveled the building, it had the collateral effect of involving the traffic and people who were passing by. Cars came to an instant halt on the street, and many were abandoned as drivers and passengers left them, running away in panic. A large, billowing cloud of smoke rolled down the street, and many thought they were seeing a repeat of the attack of 9/11.

More pedestrians began running in off the street to escape the noxious smoke.

"Down!" the man at the counter shouted. "Everyone get down!"

Mabel, the man at the end of the counter, and all the recent arrivals dived to the floor and covered their heads as, outside, men and women ran by screaming.

Through all of this, Pogue remained seated at his table, calmly drinking his coffee and eating his pie. He felt a tremendous sense of relief and satisfaction. He had done the job for one hundred thousand dollars up front, and now, having successfully completed the job, he would receive another one hundred thousand dollars. That was more money than he had ever seen in his life.

Finishing his coffee, he walked across the café floor, stepping over the prostrate forms of those who had come in to take cover. Mabel was lying behind the counter, with her hands over her head. He leaned over the counter to look down at her.

"You say you get off at seven?" Pogue asked calmly.

"What?" Mabel replied, her voice on the verge of panic.

"Seven," Pogue said. "You say you get off at seven? How would you like to go to Atlantic City with me?"

"What? No!" Mabel said. "No, are you crazy? Don't you know what just happened?"

"Yeah, the Harriet Clayton Campaign Headquarters building just blew up. I hope the bitch was in it. So, you don't want to go to Atlantic City?"

"No! No, you're crazy!"

"Okay, just thought I'd ask. Here's for the pie and coffee," he said, leaving the money on the counter.

Pogue was going to go to Atlantic City and gamble.

Never before had he had enough money to gamble with the high rollers. This time he did.

Harriet held the phone to her ear. "Answer the phone, bitch," Harriet said irritably. Finally, she snapped her cell phone shut.

"You can't get anyone?" Henry Norton asked. Harriet and Henry were in the backseat of a Cadillac provided by the airport limousine service.

"No," Harriet said.

"That's odd. I wonder what's wrong," Henry said.

"What's wrong? Nothing is wrong. It's just that you have hired a bunch of no-account ignorant assholes who are too lazy to answer the phone, that's all. If LaTisha can't at least make sure the phones are answered, then what the hell good is she? I'm going to fire her black ass just as soon as we get there."

"You don't want to do that," Henry suggested. "She's one of the best there is at this business, and you know it. She worked Eddies' campaigns for Vice President and his Presidential campaign."

"Yeah, well, when you think about it, that's not that much of an endorsement, is it? I mean, Eddie did lose, after all."

"Yes, but through no fault of LaTisha's," Eddie reminded her. "You don't want to fire her."

"The hell I don't. She's getting a little too uppity, if you ask me."

"Try her cell phone. Maybe all the other phones are tied up."

Harriet opened her phone and punched in some more numbers, then with a sigh of disgust, ended the call. "Out of area," she said. "Which means she has it turned off. God, she is worthless."

"I'm sure there is a reasonable explanation," Henry said.

"Oh, yes, you would say that. You're just trying to cover your ass for hiring her in the first place."

"I've never seen traffic this congested," Henry said, changing the subject. "It's hardly moving."

"That's why I'm trying to call LaTisha. I want her to make sure the reporter doesn't leave before we get there." She lowered the window that separated the driver from the passengers. "Driver, can't you get us out of this mess? Find another route."

"I've been on the horn checking it with all the other drivers in our service, Senator, and they are reporting that it is like this everywhere."

"It is? Well, I wonder what the hell is going on. Is there a parade or something? And if so, why wasn't I told about it?"

"No, ma'am, there's no parade," the driver answered. "But there was some sort of explosion downtown."

"Explosion? What sort of explosion? Where?"

"I don't know, Senator. All I know is there was an explosion downtown."

Harriet put the window up again, then leaned back in her seat. "Well, shit," she said. "There's no way we'll get there in time now. It looks like I'm going to miss that interview."

"I'm sure there will be another opportunity," Henry said. "I wonder what the explosion was. You don't think it was some sort of terrorist attack, do you?"

"I hope it was," Harriet said.

"What? You don't mean that."

"Yes, I do mean it. Look, I'm not saying I wanted it to happen, but as long as there was some explosion downtown anyway, I hope it was a terrorist attack. That, coming on top of the thing in Dallas and the bombing in Chicago and St. Louis, will just about prove that the President has completely lost control of everything."

"That may be true, but to *wish* for a terrorist attack?" Henry shook his head slowly. "You are a hard and calloused woman, Harriet."

"Yes, well, it will never be said that I don't have a pair of balls."

Henry looked shocked for a moment; then he laughed, and Harriet laughed with him.

Harriet's cell phone rang.

"Well, thank God," she said. "LaTisha must've finally gotten her lazy, black ass moving again." She opened her phone. "It's about time you called," she said by way of answering.

"Harriet, Thank God you are okay," a familiar, almost-hoarse-sounding voice said. This was her husband, the former Vice President and unsuccessful Presidential candidate in the previous election.

"Of course I'm okay," Harriet replied flatly. "Why the hell shouldn't I be okay?"

"You mean you haven't heard?"

"Heard what, Eddie? Get to the point, please."

"Your headquarters in Newark has just been bombed. It's on the TV and radio, but they aren't releasing all the details yet."

"My headquarters?" Harriet asked, surprised. "But no, that's impossible. Why would the terrorists attack my headquarters? I'm the only candidate willing to negotiate with them, for chrissake. What the hell? Don't those bastards ever read the newspapers?"

"Would you like to have a casualty report?" Eddie asked.

"Casualty report?"

Until this moment, Harriet hadn't even thought about the possibility of casualties.

"Oh, yes," she said, almost as an afterthought. "What about the casualties?"

"They are said to be heavy," Eddie said. "Including several killed."

"That's a shame," Harriet said. "You don't know who was killed, do you? Oh, never mind, I'll get a report from LaTisha as soon as I get there."

"That won't be possible."

"Why not? The police aren't going to keep me from talking to LaTisha."

"LaTisha was killed in the blast," Eddie said.

"LaTisha is dead?" Harriet asked. For once, the steely edge was gone from her voice and she sounded almost childlike. "Who . . . who would do such a thing?"

"Where are you now?" Eddie asked.

"I'm not sure exactly where we are. Somewhere between the airport and downtown. We are hung up in traffic."

"Listen, do you want me to come to you? Because I'll be glad to."

"No, I don't think so," Harriet said. "You probably wouldn't be able to get through anyway. I have no idea how long we are going to be stuck here."

"All right. Call me if you need me."

The hard edge came back into Harriet's voice. "I haven't needed you for twenty years, Eddie. What makes you think I would need you now?" she asked. "I have to go."

Harriet punched the phone off without saying good-bye.

New York, New York

Former Vice President Eddie Clayton and Senator Harriet Clayton owned two houses, one in Georgetown and one in Newark, New Jersey. In addition, they kept an apartment on Central Park West in New York because Eddie Clayton had a office in Manhattan. The former Vice President was a political consultant, and he commanded rather large fees for showing up at political fund-raising events.

Although the two managed to be seen together for photo ops, they were living apart, ostensibly because Harriet was on the campaign trail, though that was a convenient excuse for them to exercise what was really their choice.

Eddie was living in the Manhattan apartment, and had made the phone call from there. He hung up, then stared at the phone for a moment. There was no love lost between them, and hadn't been for some time. They maintained the façade of marriage because it was politically expedient to do so.

He was glad Harriet wasn't in her headquarters when it was bombed. On the other hand, if she had been hurt or, God forbid, killed, there would have been such a groundswell of sympathetic support for him that the nomination would have been his for the asking. For just a moment, he enjoyed the thought, even though he knew such enjoyment was evil.

Eddie had been so narrowly defeated in the last election that he had been considering running again, but was surprised and even felt a little betrayed when his wife announced her own plans before he could. What angered him even more about her announcement was that she hadn't even consulted with him beforehand. It also upset him that Henry Norton, who had been his campaign manager during his own failed attempt to become President, was now Harriet's campaign manager.

Eddie hadn't even asked about Henry. He hoped the son of a bitch was in the headquarters building when it blew up.

Ginger Alexander came into the living room then. She was wearing a hip-length dressing gown and was running a brush through her hair.

"Is Harriet okay?" she asked.

"Yes," Eddie replied.

"Good. I'm glad she wasn't hurt."

Eddie compared the sharp-edged voice of his wife with the soft, sexual invitation that was always in Ginger's voice. He remembered his first time with her. It had been while he was still Vice President.

Ginger Alexander looked sweet and innocent, but it became obvious, soon after she came to work in Eddie Clayton's office, that she wasn't innocent. She was overtly sexual around him, letting him know in every way she could that she was available. One day she came into his office wearing a ridiculously short skirt and no panties. Conveniently dropping something on the floor in front of his desk, she bent over to pick it up, making certain that he got an eyeful.

While still bent over, Ginger looked around at Eddie to check his reaction.

"Do you like what you see?" she asked.

"Who wouldn't?" Eddie answered.

Straightening up, Ginger smiled. "Well, I like to please. Oh, can I ask your opinion on something?"

"Sure."

Ginger pulled up her skirt. "As you can see, I've shaved my pubes. Do you think it makes me look too young?"

"How, uh, how old are you, honey?" Eddie asked. His tongue was thick and his breathing shallow.

"I'm nineteen, but everyone says that I don't look any older than fifteen. I guess shaving my pubes makes it even worse, huh?"

"Worse? No, that's not a term I would use," Eddie said. "I think it, uh, you are very attractive."

"Do you find me desirable?"

"Desirable? Yes, of course."

"Desirable enough for you to have sex with me?"

Eddie cleared his throat. "Let me get this straight. Are you asking me to have sex with you?"

"Yes," Ginger said. "I mean, you can do it, can't you? Everything works?"

Eddie laughed. "Yes, everything works. Sometimes I wish it didn't."

"So, do you want to have sex with me?"

"Honey, are you sure you know what you are getting into?" Eddie asked her. "You have to understand that there's no future in it for you."

"I'm not looking for a future, I'm looking for excitement," Ginger said.

"Are you going to go see her?" Ginger asked, her question bringing Eddie back to the present.

"No."

"Is she going to come here?"

"Lord, no. She won't be going anywhere for a while. She'll probably be locked up in traffic until midnight." He laughed. "I hope she has to pee."

Eighteen

New Orleans, Louisiana

Linda Marsh's red lipstick and fingernail polish perfectly matched her red-plastic earrings, necklace, and bracelet. She was wearing a white blouse with large red polka dots and a short, black skirt, and sat at a table in a Chili's restaurant in New Orleans. A nicely dressed man approached the table.

"*Señorita Valdez, es bueno de usted venire,*" he said with a friendly smile.

"*Gracias, pero prefiero hablar inglés aquí, en América,*" Linda replied. "Thank you, but I prefer to speak English here, in America," she repeated, saying the words with a thick Spanish accent. "I want to practice English for my new country."

"But of course. And you are doing very well," the man said. "My name is Asa Todaro."

"Are you to be my American husband, Señor Todaro?" Linda asked.

Todaro laughed. "No, and such is the pity too, for you are a beautiful woman."

Linda smiled, and showed proper embarrassment at the flattery.

"Have you had your lunch?"

"No."

"Suppose we have lunch, then I will take you to the next place."

"I will have a steak," Linda said.

Todaro laughed. "Very well, a steak it will be."

Newark, New Jersey

When the traffic finally thinned enough to allow them to get out of the gridlock, Harriet's driver took them to her headquarters. The street was cordoned off about two blocks from the headquarters building and uniformed policemen were directing the cars away.

"I can't go through," the driver said.

"Nonsense. Drive on through," Harriet said.

Ignoring the policeman's order to turn aside, the driver pulled around the barricade and started on down the street.

"Halt!" the policeman shouted. "Halt or I will shoot!"

"My God, he's going to shoot us!" Henry said. "Stop the car!"

The driver stopped and three policemen, all with guns drawn, raced toward the car.

"Get out of the vehicle now!" one of the cops shouted. "Get out of the car with your hands over your head!"

The driver opened the door and stepped out, holding his hands up. Neither Harriet nor Henry exited the car.

"You two in the backseat! Out, now!"

The door opened and Harriet got out of the car. Recognizing her at once, the policemen lowered their weapons. "Senator Clayton?" one of them said.

"What's the idea of threatening to shoot me?" Harriet asked angrily. "Do you know I could not only have your badge, I could have you put in prison for threatening a United States Senator?"

"I'm sorry, ma'am. But when your driver didn't stop, we were afraid it might be another bomber."

"Do bombers drive around in chauffeured Cadillac limousines?" Harriet asked.

The three policemen holstered their pistols. "No, ma'am," one of them said. "Not generally."

"Now that you have recognized me, may we drive on to my headquarters?"

"You won't be able to go more than another block," the policeman said. "The blast also caught several cars and they are blocking the street."

"I can walk up then?"

"Yes, ma'am, but I'd better have one of my men escort you," the officer replied. "James?"

"Yes, Sergeant."

"Escort Senator Clayton and her party up to the site."

"I have no further need for the driver," Harriet said. "Can he go?"

"Yes," the police sergeant said. "Turn your car around and go back out the way you came in."

"Okay, thanks."

"Oh, driver, next time you come to a police roadblock, I'd suggest you stop, no matter who you have in the car."

"Right," the driver said.

Harriet watched as the driver backed up, turned around, then drove back through the barricade.

"This way, ma'am," the young policeman who was assigned to escort her said.

At about that time another car came up to the barricade, stopped, and two men got out and sprinted around the barricade toward Harriet.

"Halt!" the police sergeant shouted at them, reaching for his pistol.

"No! They are my Secret Service Agents!" Harriet said, stopping the policeman. Then, to the agents: "A couple of fine bodyguards you two are. Where the hell were you?"

"We got separated in the traffic jam," one of them said. "I told you we were supposed to ride in the car with you."

"I don't want you in my face all the time," Harriet said. "Come on, let's go see what's left of my headquarters building."

With the young policeman leading the way, Harriet, Henry, and her two bodyguards picked their way up the street, stepping over the debris of shattered windows and car parts. There were at least fifteen cars in the block immediately in front of the building, and all were burned-out hunks of rust-colored metal. A few still had tires, but in most cases the tires had burned away so that the gutted cars were sitting on bare wheel rims.

What had been her campaign headquarters was now nothing but a pile of charred masonry and blackened, still-smoking wood frames. The buildings on either side of her building were nearly as badly damaged. At least a dozen firemen were poking around in the rubble, wearing helmets and protective coats.

"No civilians," one of the firemen on the scene shouted, waving his hands and coming toward them.

"This is Senator Clayton," Officer James said. "This was her headquarters."

"Oh," the fireman said. He touched the brim of his hat. "I'm real sorry about this, ma'am."

"Do you know how it happened?" Harriet asked.

"There is what's left of a truck out back," the fireman said. "It looks like that's how the bomb got here. The young lady over there saw it." He pointed to a young woman, in her early twenties, who was standing across the street, wearing a blanket around her shoulders and looking on in shock at the devestation.

"Who is that?" Harriet asked.

"Her name is Rempke. Shirley Rempke. She's one of your workers."

"One of my workers?"

"Yes, ma'am."

"Is it all right if I go talk to her?"

"Yes, ma'am. Go right ahead."

Harriet and the others crossed the street. "Miss Rempke?" she said.

Seeing Harriet, Shirley started to cry. "Oh, Senator Clayton, it's all my fault," she said. "I saw the truck and I thought it was rather strange being back there, but I didn't say anything. I didn't warn anybody."

"You didn't know the truck was carrying a bomb, did you?" Harry asked.

"No, but . . ."

"Then it is nonsense to say that it is your fault."

"How is it that you weren't hurt?" Harriet asked.

"Miss Waters sent me down to the office supply store to get a box of manila folders," Shirley said. "It's down there." She pointed. "I was just going into it when I heard the explosion. The minute I heard it, I knew," she said. "I just knew." She began crying again.

"We've found another body!" one of the firemen called, and several of the other firemen hurried over to lend a hand in the extraction.

"I wonder how many they've pulled out so far," Harriet said.

"Eighty-six," Shirley answered. "Only ten alive, but they were either in the adjoining buildings, or in one of the cars. Nobody from the headquarters has been found alive."

"LaTisha?"

"Miss Waters was one of the first ones they pulled from the rubble," Shirley said. "She's dead. Like . . . like all the others."

* * *

Fountain Hills, Arizona

"*Caramba!* The man who is to be my American husband lives here?" Linda asked as she stepped out of the airport limo that had brought her and Asa Todaro from the airport in Phoenix.

"Yes."

"What a beautiful place. Is he rich?"

Todaro laughed. "Yes, he is very rich. Now, aren't you glad you responded to the website, Miss Valdez?"

"*Sí!* Very much so! Oh, is that my new husband?" she asked, pointing to a man who was coming from the house.

"No, that is Baldwin Carter. He is an employee."

"Come in. Mr. Bustamante is expecting you," Baldwin said, leading the way back into the house.

As Baldwin waited in the great room with Linda, Todaro walked into Bustamante's office.

"Well, you asked me to bring the next good-looking woman to you," Todaro said. "And that is exactly what I did. She's waiting out in the great room."

"She'd better be good-looking, Todaro. I mean damn good-looking," Bustamante said.

"Wait until you see her," Baldwin replied. "I swear to you, she's about the prettiest woman I've ever seen."

"And you say she is from Colombia?"

"Yes," Todaro said. He smiled. "I thought you might find that especially appealing."

"It depends," Bustamante said.

"Depends? Depends on what? I already told you how beautiful she is."

"Yes, but danger often comes in beautiful packages. What if the Medellin has planted her here? What if she is an assassin?"

"Ha!" Todaro said. "She might be a lot of things, but there's no way she is an assassin."

Taking an atomizer from his pocket, Bustamante sprayed his throat with a breath-freshener; then he walked out to the great room where Baldwin and a young woman were sitting. As he approached, the young woman smiled and stood. Bustamante smiled back. Todaro was right about one thing. This was a beautiful woman, so beautiful that it nearly took his breath away.

"Do you speak English?"

"*Sí,*" Linda answered, then she laughed nervously. "I mean yes."

"And your name is Valdez?"

"Yes, Pilar Valdez," Linda said.

"I am Arturo Pablo Bustamante."

Linda gasped, then took a step back and curtsied. "You, you are Arturo Bustamante?"

"Arturo Pablo Bustamante," Bustamante said, emphasizing the Pablo. "Arturo was my father."

"My father has told me tales of him. Arturo was a hero of our nation. Truly, you must also be a hero! I am honored!"

Pablo laughed, then turned to Todaro. "You are right," he said. "She will do."

Code Name Team Headquarters

"She's in," Don said. He handed an e-mail message to John. "I've already decoded it."

"I am inside, and have evidence to support the theory that Bustamante and Jahmshidi are working together."

* * *

Alexandria, Virginia

Slipping just out of focus in the early evening rain, the city resembled a painting by Monet. On one side of Marshall Avenue, the rush-hour taillights painted a long, liquid smear of red, while the cars' headlights drew a white streak coming in the opposite direction. Pink and green and blue and orange neon lights added their own wet, glimmering hues to the night.

In an apartment on the seventeenth floor of Preston Court Arms, *"luxury apartment-living for the discriminating,"* six people were meeting. The atmosphere was purposely kept casual, but the agenda was very serious.

"We have gone to the government of Sitarkistan to ask that they surrender Jahmshidi Mehdi to us," Tom Harold said. "But they refused."

Tom Harold was an operative for the CIA. When John had been a member of the CIA, Tom Harold had worked with him. In fact, John had been Tom's mentor. Now Tom was often the go-between between the Code Name Team and the CIA.

"So what do you do next?" John asked.

"We had planned to go to the United Nations to ask for a resolution demanding that Sitarkistan surrender Jahmshidi to us or face military action."

"You had planned?" Jennifer asked. "Meaning that you aren't going to?"

"France has said that they will veto any resolution calling for military action," Tom said.

"So, where does that leave us? With unilateral military action?" John asked.

Tom walked back over to the bar and poured himself another drink.

"I wish it was that easy," he said. "But the truth is, even if we have enough votes to get it through Congress, and

I think we do, though it would just barely pass, we would be in a no-win situation. Senator Clayton is promising a filibuster if it comes up, and she would make her opposition to it the centerpiece in her Presidential campaign. That would split the country right down the middle. We can't afford to go into any military action without overwhelming support from the people."

"So you aren't going to ask for a Congressional resolution."

"No, for to do so would be counterproductive," Tom said.

"That doesn't leave a lot of options," Jennifer said.

"I know. And now you see our dilemma."

"So what are we going to do? Just let Jahmshidi and Bustamante pick us off at will?" Mike asked.

"No, we had something else in mind."

"What is that?" John asked.

"The President was hoping you could handle it," Tom said. He took the Code Name Team in with a wave of his hand. "And when I say you, I mean all of you," he added.

"Handle it how?" John asked. "What I mean is, what sort of restrictions will be imposed on us?"

Tom took a swallow of his drink and stared at them for a long moment before he answered.

"None," he said. "We want you to make them both go away. Bustamante and Jahmshidi."

"Make them go away," John repeated.

"With extreme prejudice," Tom said.

Fountain Hills, Arizona

"I'm not exactly sure what he has planned, but it has something to do with the Democratic National Convention in Chicago. I know he plans to disrupt it in some way, perhaps violently."

Linda had just tapped the "send" button when she felt something hard and cold being pressed against the back of her head.

"What did you just send?"

Turning in her chair, Linda saw Bustamante holding a gun on her. She smiled broadly.

"Why, it was just a letter to my parents," she said. "I was telling them how wonderful it is here with you."

"Let me tell you why I know you are lying," Bustamante replied calmly. "When you looked at me just now, you smiled. If you were a poor, ignorant girl from Colombia, you wouldn't be smiling now. You would be terrified."

"I am terrified," Linda said.

"No. You are collected. Open the letter you just sent."

Linda opened the letter, and Bustamante looked at the screen.

"What the hell is this?" he asked. "This is in code! You send e-mail to your parents in code?"

Linda looked at the screen as well. "So it would appear," she said, calmly.

"Who the hell are you?" Bustamante asked, angrily.

"Well, I'm not your ordinary piece of ass, I'll tell you that," Linda replied.

"Bitch!" Bustamante shouted, bringing the barrel of the pistol down sharply on the side of Linda's head.

She went down.

Chicago, Illinois

McCormick Place was decorated for the Democratic National Convention with huge flags and red, white, and blue streamers and bunting hanging over every entrance. Security was exceptionally heavy, not only at every entrance, but inside the building as well, along the corridors and in the great hall itself. Outside, police snipers were in position all around the building, keeping a watchful eye on the proceedings.

In response to Linda's e-mail warning that something was being planned for the convention in Chicago, John and Jennifer had managed to be hired as security consultants. In that capacity, they were free to roam anywhere in the building, and they came down onto the floor to look at the big stage where all the events would take place.

"Do you think she is actually going to get the nomination?" Jennifer asked.

"She has enough delegates committed to her to get it on the first ballot," John answered.

"How has she managed to pull the wool over everyone's eyes?"

Near the stage, a beeping sound cautioned everyone that a pickup truck was backing up. The back of the truck was loaded with an array of huge speakers, part of the stage setting for a band that called itself Confusion Illusion. Confusion Illusion was one of the hottest bands in the country, and it was considered a coup to get them to perform in the opening ceremonies of the convention, though in truth, nearly half of the delegates had never heard of them.

When the truck stopped, the driver opened the door and stepped out onto the convention hall floor. This was about the biggest gathering of people Dexter Pogue had ever seen. And every damn one of them was a liberal, willing to sell out the rights of the people in exchange for votes from the blacks, the Hispanics, and the poor.

He was disappointed when the bomb he set off at the Clayton headquarters didn't kill her. However, the person he was working for, and Pogue had no idea who that might be, was pleased with what he had done in Newark, and hired him to do it again, but on a much grander scale, at the national convention.

Pogue was happy with the arrangement, not only because it meant more money, but also because it would give him a second chance at Harriet Clayton. He didn't realize until he reached Chicago and started planning the operation that Harriet would not be on the floor. Harriet was one of the candidates seeing the nomination, so by tradition, she would not be present until after the nominating process was completed.

As Pogue began unloading the speakers, some of which were as large as he was, a couple of security officers came over to check him out.

"Ain't no need to check on nothin'," Pogue said. "These here is speakers for the band, and they done been checked."

"Good. Then we'll check them again," one of the security officers said. He had a bomb-sniffing dog, and the dog went to work.

Pogue folded his arms across his chest and leaned back against the truck watching as the dog worked. After a few minutes, the dog lost interest and turned away.

"Okay," the security guard said.

"Look at the size of those speakers," John said, nodding toward the stage. "Lord, can you just imagine the noise they will put out."

"Not noise, music," Jennifer replied.

"No, it's noise. Compared to this, a car hitting a wall at fifty miles an hour would be music."

Jennifer laughed.

As John and Jennifer continued to wander around the building, Pogue set up the speakers. One of the speakers began squealing, and the noise was loud and very irritating. He disconnected that speaker and put it back on the truck.

"You hungry?" John asked. "Let's get a hot dog."

"A hot dog, is it? Wow, you really know how to wine and dine a girl, don't you?" Jennifer teased.

They walked to one of the vending areas, where John bought a couple of hot dogs and two coffees. They were at the condiments table when the little pickup truck drove back toward the stage, with the speaker in the back.

"I hope he got the squeal fixed," John said.

"Yeah, that was pretty irritating," Jennifer said. "He must not have been able to fix the other speaker. That's not the same speaker he took out of here," she said.

John was just about to take a bite of his hot dog, but he brought it back down and looked at Jennifer.

"He switched speakers?"

"Yes."

"What if you wanted to get something in here without it having it checked?"

"You'd bring something in here that was already checked," Jennifer said.

"Or at least something that everyone assumed was already checked," John replied. "Let's go take a look."

Leaving their hot dogs, John and Jennifer started toward the stage, reaching there just as the driver climbed up onto the back of the truck.

"Hold it," John called out. "I need to take a look at the speaker."

"It's already been checked," Pogue said.

"Then you won't mind if we check it again."

"No, I don't mind," Pogue said. "Come on up and have a look."

As John started to climb up onto the back of the truck, Pogue reached under a piece of canvas and came up with a pistol. He brought the pistol up and aimed it at John from point-blank range.

John heard a gunshot, then saw a look of surprise

cross Pogue's face. Pogue dropped his pistol, looked down at the hole in his chest, then dropped to his knees. Just before he collapsed, he reached out and did something to the speaker.

"John, he armed it!" Jennifer shouted. Jennifer was standing on the floor about six feet away from the truck, the gun still smoking in her hand. It had been her shot that took Pogue out.

Ripping open the cloth cover off the speaker, John saw the bomb, and a digital readout.

"How much time?" Jennifer called.

"Less than thirty seconds!" John replied.

Without a second thought, John jumped into the truck, put it in gear, and started forward, squealing the tires on the concrete floor as he did so. He had no clear plan in mind as he started driving; he wanted only to get the truck out of the building. But a quick glance toward the exit told him that he would never make it in time.

He turned away from the exit and started toward the wall. Ahead of him was a huge floor-to-ceiling window. John accelerated.

At the last minute, John opened the door to the truck and jumped out onto the cement floor. He hit and rolled painfully, but the truck kept going, crashing through the window.

From the window it was a drop of some forty feet to the parking lot below, but the truck exploded almost as soon as it smashed through the glass, the flash of the explosion lighting up the exhibition hall. The force of the blast broke three or four other windows, in addition to the one the truck itself had taken out.

Jennifer ran to John, who was getting up slowly.

"John! Are you all right?" she asked.

"Yeah," John replied. He looked around. "Where's the driver?"

"He was still in the back of the truck," Jennifer said.

Nineteen

Fountain Hills, Arizona

Baldwin Carter hung up the telephone. "The helicopter will be here for you in a few minutes," he said.

"Good," Bustamante replied. "What about Jahmshidi?"

"The latest information I have is that he will be arriving at the island today, along with several of his followers."

"Followers," Bustamante scoffed. "His martyrs brigade, you mean. I don't mind telling you, it's going to be a little spooky being around a bunch of people who are planning to blow themselves up."

"They are men of deep conviction," Baldwin said.

"They are insane," Bustamante said. "But if those dumb assholes want to kill themselves, let 'em, it's no sweat off my balls. And letting him use the island as a base for his operations is putting Jahmshidi in my debt."

Asa Todaro, who was still Bustamante's house guest, stuck his head into Bustamante's office then.

"Pablo, there's something on TV I think you should see," he said.

"What?"

"Something happened in Chicago."

"Ha!" Bustamante said, smiling broadly. "You damn right something happened in Chicago."

Todaro shook his head. "No," he said. "It's not quite what you think."

"What? What do you mean?"

"Come see for yourself," Todaro said. "It's all over the tube."

Bustamante and Baldwin followed Todaro back into the great room, where he had been watching television.

News of the bomb at the convention in Chicago had hit all the wire services and networks and was the biggest story of the day. As it happened, one of the networks was getting their cameras set up for the convention coverage, and they managed to get pictures of the incident. The image of the truck crashing though the window, then exploding immediately thereafter, was shown again and again.

"Identified as Ron Tracey, the man who drove the truck through the window had been hired by McCormick Place as a security consultant. Authorities say that his quick action saved many lives," the TV announcer said. "But the man they are now calling the shy hero would not grant an interview, so this is the only picture we have of him."

The camera did a freeze frame of John shortly after he stood, clearly showing his face.

"Ron Tracey my ass," Bustamante said, pointing toward the screen. "That's the same guy who tried to bust my ass in Los Angeles. That's John Barrone."

"If it's John Barrone, then that means the Code Name Team is involved," Todaro said.

"How do you know?"

"Because he is the head of them."

"I don't understand. Does the Code Name Team hire themselves out as security consultants or something?" Baldwin asked.

Todaro shook his head. "No. If the Code Name Team

was there, it's because they knew something was going down."

"How could they know unless . . ." Bustamante began, then stopped in mid-sentence. "She's part of them," he said.

"Who's part of them?" Todaro asked.

"That bitch you brought in here. She's part of the Code Name Team. She has to be."

Linda was handcuffed to the bed when Bustamante came into her bedroom.

"What did you tell them?" he demanded angrily.

Linda's beautiful features were distorted by the beating she had taken. One eye was discolored and nearly shut, there was a bruise on her cheek, and her lip was cut and swollen.

"I don't know what you are talking about," Linda replied. "What did I tell who?"

"Don't lie to me, bitch! You know what and who I'm talking about. I'm talking about the Code Name Team."

"Oh, that," Linda said dryly.

"That? Then you admit it?"

"I don't admit anything."

"I don't know how you told them about Chicago, but somehow you did."

"What's the matter, Mr. Bustamante? Did somebody piss on your parade in Chicago?"

Bustamante drew back his hand to hit her again, and Linda flinched, bracing for the blow. But to her relief, he lowered his hand in frustration.

"I'll take care of you later. You just wait."

Linda pulled on her handcuffs, which were attached to the head of the bed. "Okay," she said sarcastically. "I'll just wait here."

Returning to the great room, John found Baldwin and Todaro waiting for him.

"What did she say?" Baldwin asked.

"What did she say? What could she say? She's the one who warned them about Chicago. I never should have let her use the computer. 'I want to e-mail my parents,' she said." He looked over at Baldwin. "I blame you for that. You should have paid more attention to what she was doing."

"I'm sorry," Baldwin said. "But I have to walk a fine line around here. I've made it my business, ever since coming to work for you, not to invade your privacy."

"Yeah, I know. That way you can maintain your credible deniability. But you aren't going to be able to hang on to that much longer. Not after this trip to the island."

"I know," Baldwin said. "But the situation has changed, and I am prepared for it."

"Yes, well, that still leaves us with a problem," Bustamante said.

"It doesn't have to be a problem," Todaro said.

"What do you mean it doesn't have to be a problem?"

"I mean it doesn't have to be a problem because I'll take care of it."

Bustamante looked at Todaro for a moment, then nodded. The sound of the approaching helicopter invaded their conversation.

"All right, you take care of it," Bustamante said, pointing at Todaro. "Come on, Baldwin, let's go."

"You go on, sir," Baldwin said. "I think I can better serve you by staying here."

"What do you mean? What are you going to do?"

Baldwin looked pointedly at Todaro. "I may have to clean up after Mr. Todaro. I'm not sure he can handle the situation."

"What do you mean I can't handle the situation, you little faggot?" Todaro responded angrily.

"Oh, I'm quite sure you can kill her," Baldwin said. "But can you do it in a way that doesn't leave Mr. Bustamante liable?"

"Good point, Baldwin," Bustamante said. "Maybe you had better stay and clean up after him."

"You think I can't do this without it involving you?" Todaro asked.

"Maybe you can and maybe you can't," Bustamante said. "But I know Baldwin can. He is the most dependable man I've ever had around me."

"Why, thank you, sir," Baldwin said. "Coming from you, that is indeed a compliment."

"But Baldwin, are you sure you want to do this? If you stay here you'll be a party to murder," Bustamante warned. "That certainly goes beyond giving up credible deniability."

"I realize that, but as the saying goes, in for a penny, in for a pound," Baldwin replied. "And as long as this woman is alive she is a threat, not only to you, but to all of us."

"That's true," Bustamante said. The sound of the helicopter was very loud now.

"You had better go, sir," Baldwin said.

Bustamante nodded. "Right," he said. "I'll be back in a few days." Bustamante started outside to meet his ride.

"Have a good trip, sir," Baldwin called after him. He and Todaro went over to the window to watch as Bustamante climbed into the helicopter. The pilot pulled pitch, and dust, dirt, and tiny rocks flew up from the rotor wash as the craft lifted from the ground. It poised for a moment on its ground cushion; then the nose dipped down and started forward until it reached transitional lift and began its climb away from the property.

"Have a good trip, sir," Todaro mimicked. "If you had

your nose any further up his ass, it would break your neck every time he made a turn."

"It does not hurt to pay your employer his due respect," Baldwin said.

"Come on, let's get this over with," Todaro said, pulling his pistol from his holster. "By the way, when you said you were going to clean up after me, that's exactly what you're going to do. After I shoot the bitch, I'm finished with it."

"I understand," Baldwin said.

When they went into the room where they were keeping Linda, she was still handcuffed to the bed.

"Good-bye, bitch," Todaro said, pointing the pistol at her.

"Wait!" Baldwin said.

Todaro lowered his gun. "Wait for what?"

"Don't shoot her in here. If you do, the police can trace it back to Mr. Bustamante."

"That's your problem. You're the one that's supposed to clean up."

"You have no idea how sophisticated the CSI units are today. Even if you think all the blood has been washed away, there will still be traces."

"Then what do you suggest we do?"

"Take her outside," he said. "There's a gully out back. We can kill her and bury her in the same place."

"All right. But let's not take all day doing this. I need to catch a plane back to New Orleans."

Baldwin took a key from his pocket and released Linda's handcuffs from the bed.

"Put your hands behind you," he said. When Linda complied, he snapped the cuffs shut.

"Let's go," Todaro said, waving his pistol toward the door.

"No, not that way," Baldwin said. "It's shorter through here."

Baldwin opened the door that led from the bedroom directly out onto the pool. They were about halfway across the pool deck when Linda suddenly spun around and kicked. Her kick sent Baldwin sprawling.

"Bitch!" Todaro shouted. He shot at Linda, but missed when Linda leaped over a planter and squatted behind it. Looking around for an escape route, she saw that the patio was completely enclosed by a high brick wall. The only exit was a gate at the far end of the pool. She thought about trying to make it, but knew she couldn't.

"Well, now, look at this," Todaro said. "You're all dressed up with no place to go." He laughed, then took slow and deliberate aim.

Linda closed her eyes and waited for the inevitable. She heard the shot, but felt nothing. Then she heard two more shots in quick succession and, curious, opened her eyes to see what was going on.

She saw Todaro fall back into the pool. He floated away from the pool's edge, his arms spread out, his head back, his blood dyeing the water red.

Baldwin was down on one knee, also bleeding. He lowered the pistol he had used to shoot Todaro.

"Come here, let me unlock your cuffs," Baldwin said, his voice strained with pain.

Linda hurried to him, turned her back, and presented her wrists so he could free her. Then, freed, she looked to his gunshot wound.

"I'm going to call an ambulance," she said.

"No!" Baldwin replied. He coughed, and when he did, blood came from his mouth. "There's no time for that."

Linda began pressing down on the wound, trying to stem the flow of blood.

"My real name is Amon Cooper," he said. "I'm a DEA agent, working undercover."

"You should've told me earlier," Linda said. "We could've worked together."

"I didn't know who you were," the dying agent said. "I didn't know if you could be trusted." He coughed again. "I still don't know, but I have no choice. I have to trust you."

"I've got to get something to use as a bandage," Linda said.

"No, there's no time! Listen to me!"

"All right."

Bustamante has cut a deal with Jahmshidi Mehdi to let him use the island as a staging area. Jahmshidi is bringing about twenty suicide bombers with him. He's going to let them loose on our country."

"Where?" Linda asked. "Where is this staging area?"

"It's . . . angel . . . angel," the agent said. He tried one more time, then, with one last gasp of breath, he died. But not before telling her what she needed to know.

Sky Harbor Airport, Phoenix

The whole team was there. John Barrone, Jennifer Barnes, Linda Marsh, Chris Vogel, and Mike Rojas had been joined by Paul Brewer, Lana Henry, and Bob Garrett, freshly returned from missions of their own.

They were sitting on canvas seats in the back of a Caribou, and because they were all heavily armed, and wearing battle dress utilities, they could've been a military unit preparing for a mission.

Paul Brewer was the only black on the team. He was in his forties, a powerfully built man who had starred in the Canadian Football League. Before joining the Code Name Team, Paul had been with the Border Patrol.

Lana Henry was the third woman on the team, and like Linda and Jennifer, was exceptionally skilled in martial arts.

Bob Garrett was the final member of the team. Bob had been a CIA operative whose greatest skill was in his ability to blend in with practically any ethnic group.

John studied the faces of each of them as they waited. It was interesting to see how each reacted to imminent danger. Some showed an eagerness to get the show on the road; others showed a studied indifference to it. But he knew that each man and woman was ready for what was ahead of them, and he knew that he would be able to put his life on the line with all or any of them.

Don Yee, who would be flying the plane, came back from the flight operations office.

"They filed for Hermosillo," Don reported, a triumphant smile on his face.

"Hermosillo?" Bob Garrett asked. "Where is that?"

"It's in Mexico," Paul said. "Northern Sonora."

"Is there a town close by with the name angel in it?" Linda asked. "Like Angeles, or something?"

"No, not that I'm aware of," Paul replied.

"Don, you have a map of Mexico?"

"Just flight charts," Don said.

"We need a map of Mexico."

"I'll bet there's a road atlas in the terminal," Mike suggested. "I'll go get one." He stood up and started toward the tail ramp, which was still open.

"Uh, Mike," Chris called.

Mike turned toward him.

"You might want to leave your firepower behind," he said.

Mike laughed. "Yeah, good idea."

* * *

"Here it is," John said, pointing to a spot on the map. "Isla del Angel Guardián. It's over close to the Baha Peninsula."

"Any place to land?"

"Nothing on the island," John said. "But we wouldn't want to land there anyway. They'd see us coming and they'd be ready for us."

"Look, there's a little road here," Don said. "It's just across Canal De Ballenas. I can put it down there, and you won't be more than a couple of miles away by water."

"All right, Don," John said. "Let's go."

John moved up front to ride in the copilot's seat. He occupied the position not because he had a pilot's license, because he did not, but because he was the field commander for this operation.

He watched as Don went through the starting procedures until both engines were turning. Then Don took down the microphone.

"Sky Harbor Tower, this is Caribou Seven-five-seven, taxi and takeoff, please."

Tower responded, and John leaned back to get comfortable as the plane taxied away from the parking area.

Twenty

Baha California

Don made a low pass over a narrow, dirt road, then climbed back up and turned onto his downwind leg.

"Tell everyone to strap in," he said. "Here we go."

"You've got to be shitting me!" John said. "You're going to put it down there?"

"Yep."

"You'll never make it!"

"Sure I will. It'll be as easy as setting down at DFW."

"You're crazy!"

"I'm crazy? You're the one who is riding with me," Don said, chuckling as he turned onto the base leg.

John turned and looked back into the plane. "Buckle up!" he shouted. "We're landing."

"Landing where?" Jennifer said.

"Here," Chris replied, chuckling.

Don rolled out on final, then started down, flaps and gear fully extended. John sat there, holding on to the seat with both hands, feeling absolutely helpless as the airplane lost altitude and airspeed on its way down.

"Don, normally when you get close to the ground, the runway gets bigger, doesn't it?" John asked.

"Normally," Don answered.

"This one isn't getting any bigger."

Don laughed. "Do you have a puckered butt hole?" he asked.

"It's so tight you couldn't drive a straw up it with a ten-pound sledgehammer," John said.

"Good, good, puckered assholes always help," Don said.

Just before they touched down, a rabbit hopped up from a clump of grass, bounded down the road for several feet, then skittered off to one side just as the plane hit the ground.

Don reversed the props and put the engines at full power while standing on the brakes. Dust billowed up around the plane, forming a cloud that was so thick that for a moment John could see nothing. Finally, the plane stopped and the cloud of dust drifted away. When it did, John saw that they were less than ten feet away from a large outcropping of rocks and boulders.

"Piece of cake," Don said as he killed the engines.

John sat in his seat for a moment, listening to the descending hum of gyros, then, realizing he had been holding his breath, took a deep breath. He looked back into the cabin.

"All right," he said. "Off your ass and on your feet, out of the shade and into the heat."

They waited until dark; then they crossed the water in three rubber rafts, landing at the southwest end of the island. There was no moon, and the night was very dark, but all were wearing night-vision goggles that allowed them to see everything in cool shades of green.

John pointed to the two observation towers.

"They're not only manned," he said. "But they are the control points for the claymores. Chris, can you take them out from here?"

"Roger that," Chris said. Taking a kneeling position, Chris wrapped the sling around his arm to give him extra support, aimed, and fired. The flash suppressor prevented the flash of light that would normally accompany a gunshot, and the silencer made it sound like little more than a sneeze.

John was watching the occupant of the tower, and he saw him stagger back, then fall.

Chris turned his rifle toward the guide in the other tower. Ten seconds later, he was out of action as well.

"Jennifer, if we turn the claymores, can you set them off?"

"Yes," Jennifer said. "All I'll need is some commo wire, and I brought that."

"Okay, guys, let's go in," Chris said.

Running forward in a crouch, they reached the concertina wire, then cut through it. Moving more cautiously on the other side, they located three of the claymore mines, turned them, and Jennifer began stringing them so she could activate them remotely.

Reaching the processing sheds, Jennifer began planting explosives. It took her about five minutes to get all the charges set; then she came back to John.

"Ready to go," she said.

"All right," John said to the others. "Get into positions, establish interlacing fields of fire, then report."

"Ready," Chris said shortly.

"Ready," Mike offered.

One by one, the members of the team reported they were in position and ready.

"Okay, Jennifer, a little music, please," John said.

Smiling, Jenny raised up on her elbows and pointed her remote device toward the processing shed. She depressed the button and, instantly, the near end of the shed went up with a roar.

"De la alarma! Tenemos intrusos!"

"You damn straight you have intruders," Linda said quietly.

"Están ahí!" one of the guards yelled.

"No, we aren't over there, we're over here, dumb-ass," Linda said.

The first guard began firing toward the shed, which was several yards away from where the Code Name Team had taken up their positions. As soon as the first guard started shooting, the others came out to join in, so that the camp was echoing and re-echoing with gunfire. They continued to fire until most had run out of ammunition.

"Okay, take 'em out!" John shouted.

The Code Name Team opened fire and, in less than ten seconds, every exposed guard was down.

"Here come the reserves," Paul shouted, pointing back toward the guard shack. At least ten more men were running toward the compound, firing indiscriminately.

"Hold your fire!" Jenny shouted. "These are mine."

Jenny connected the two pieces of commo wire to a small generator and, when the closing guards were in position, she snapped the trigger.

The two claymore mines went off almost simultaneously, spewing fire and shrapnel in a fan-shaped pattern of death. To a man, the guards who had been in reserve went down.

Jennifer turned her attention back to the processing sheds. Once again using her remote, she set off the rest of the charges. Within moments the compound was ablaze with a dozen or more fires. But the gunfire had stopped.

"What now?" Mike asked.

"Now we find Bustamante and Jahmshidi," John said.

At that moment they heard the keening sound of a turbine engine spooling up.

"John! They're getting away in a helicopter!" Chris shouted.

"Come on! We've got to stop them!" Mike said.

The team stood up and started toward the sound of the helicopter, but as they did so, as many as twenty men suddenly burst out of one of the nearby buildings and started running toward them.

"Allah u Al-kaber!"

"Wait a minute! Hold your fire!" John shouted. "They aren't armed!"

Suddenly one of the men rushing toward them exploded, and as he did so, two more close to him exploded as well. Humming chunks of shrapnel whizzed through the air from the explosion, and though the bomber was too far away for it to have any direct effect, the Code Name Team saw bits and pieces of the nails, nuts, and bolts that were part of a suicide bomber's bomb.

"Son of a bitch!" Paul shouted. "John, they're all wearing bombs!"

"Shoot 'em!" John shouted. "Stop them before they get any closer!"

Once more the Code Name Team opened fire, this time with spectacular results. As each bullet struck one of the suicide bombers, his bomb burst in a flash of fire and flesh. With moments there was nothing left of the martyr brigade but bits and pieces of bone and tissue.

By then, the helicopter had lifted off the ground and started east, toward the sea.

"Do you have it, Paul?" John asked.

"Yes," Paul answered, taking a canvas bag down from his shoulder and handing it to John.

Almost unhurriedly, John unzipped the bag and removed the Stinger antiaircraft weapon. He assembled it, loaded it, then pointed it in the direction of the helicopter.

By now the rapidly retreating helicopter was no more than tiny flashing lights in the distant dark sky.

John pulled the trigger, there was a roar, then the missile leapt upward, riding a tail of fire. It flew far into the inky blackness of the night, going so quickly and so far that, within a couple of seconds, the missile's fiery tail was a tiny dot of light. Had it not been bright and orange, and still moving, it would have been lost amidst the stars.

Suddenly there was a large flash of brilliant white light in the heavens. Not until the helicopter was falling to earth in a widely dispersed pattern of flaming debris did the sound of the explosion hit them . . . a low, stomach-jarring thump.

Chicago, Illinois

The next day John Barrone and Tom Harold were waiting in the living room of Senator Harriet Clayton's hotel suite. After making them wait for almost fifteen minutes, Harriet came into the room.

"Mr. Barrone," she said. "I thought our last meeting established our relationship. And if memory serves, that relationship was one of mutual dislike."

"Something like that," John replied.

"And you are?" Harried asked, glancing toward Tom Harold.

"I am a friend of Mr. Barrone's," Tom said, offering no further information.

"Well, I must say that your being his friend doesn't say much for you," Harriet said. "At least in my book. Now, as I'm sure you can understand, I am a very busy woman. What can I do for you?"

"You can release your delegates and withdraw your bid for the nomination," John said.

Harriet laughed. "Are you crazy?"

"No," John said. "Not crazy. Just insistent. Withdraw from the race, release your delegates, and throw the nomination onto the convention floor."

"And just why should I do something like that?"

"Perhaps this will tell you why," John said, handing a manila folder to her.

"What is this?" Harriet asked contemptuously.

"Read it. Then decide what you are going to do. If you decide to withdraw from the race, ask for air time. But do so before ten o'clock central tomorrow morning."

Harriet glanced quickly through the folder. "My God," she said. "What is this?"

Code Name Headquarters

By a quarter to ten central time the next morning, the entire Code Name Team was assembled in the den, watching television. In what was an extremely rare occurrence, they had a guest. John had brought Tom Harold back from Chicago with him.

Don Yee came into the room with an enormous bowl of popcorn.

"Oh, Don, how nice of you to make popcorn!" Lana said.

"Oh," Don replied, mumbling through a mouthful of popcorn. "Did you want some too? I could make some more, but I might not be finished by ten."

Lana looked at the huge bowl, then chuckled. "No," she said. "I can see that you've barely got enough for yourself. Enjoy."

"You should've said something," Don replied, settling onto the couch with the popcorn in his lap. "I would've been glad to pop a little extra."

Right in the middle of the program, a graphic popped up, with the words WNN ALERT*!*

"Ladies and gentleman, this is a World News Alert," the voice-over said. "World News Network has just learned that Senator Harriet Clayton has asked for air time for an important announcement. We go now to Senator Clayton's headquarters in Chicago."

The graphic on the screen was replaced by a picture of Harriet Clayton. She was sitting at a desk with an American flag behind her. Her face was drawn-looking. She sat there for a moment, obviously waiting for a cue, then began to speak.

"My fellow Americans. When I ran for the United States Senate four years ago, I promised the voters of the great state of New Jersey that I would serve a complete term. Over the last year, however, I was urged by people from all walks of life to seek the nomination for President of the United States. Private polls conducted throughout the state of New Jersey indicated that my constituents would release me from that promise, so I undertook the campaign.

"However, the decision has never rested easily with me. Too many politicians make promises, only to be broken. I did not want to be such a politician. Therefore, effective immediately, I am freeing my delegates to cast their vote as their heart dictates. I will not seek, nor will I accept my party's nomination for President of the United States.

"Thank you, and God bless America."

"I'll be damned," Chris said. "What caused her to change her mind?"

"We handed her a report file yesterday," John said. "We asked her to read it, then to withdraw."

"You forced her to withdraw, just like that?"

"Yes. Well, we didn't. It was actually something Linda did that forced the withdrawal," John said.

"Wait a minute. Something I did made her withdraw?" Linda asked, surprised by the comment.

"Yes. You brought us all of Bustamante's hard drives, remember?" Tom Harold asked.

"Yes, of course I remember. I removed them from each of his computers before I left Fountain Hills."

"There was some very interesting information on those hard drives," Tom said. "It turns out that when Bustamante had his money-changing operation shut down in New Orleans, he found another excellent source of laundering money."

"Wait a minute. Are you going to tell me Harriet was laundering money for Bustamante?" Linda asked.

"She wasn't laundering it through her personal account," Tom said. "But her campaign was."

"Well, I'll be damned."

"So that's what was in the file you showed her?"

"Yes," Tom said. "When she realized she had been caught red-handed, she had no choice but to withdraw."

"All right!" the others said with a round of applause.

"Someday historians will thank you," Chris said. "That is, if they ever found out who did it. I can't imagine anything worse than having that woman as our President."

"I don't know," John said.

"What? John, you can't mean you think she might have made a good President?" Jennifer asked.

"Tom, do you remember her reaction when she opened the folder?"

"Yes. She realized she had been caught."

"Did she? What exactly did she say, do you remember?"

"Yes, she said something like, what is this?"

"Her exact words were, 'My God, what is this?' Not, 'How did you get this?'"

"What are you getting at, John?" Linda asked.

"I wouldn't have thought this yesterday, but I believe she may have been as surprised by that information as we were. I think it is possible that someone on her staff was responsible, and she knew nothing about it."

"Never," Mike said. "If Harriet Clayton thought somebody had stuck it to her like that, she never would've given up as easily as she did."

"Unless she had more class than any of us ever gave her credit for," John said. "And if that's true, we may have just cost our country one hell of a President."